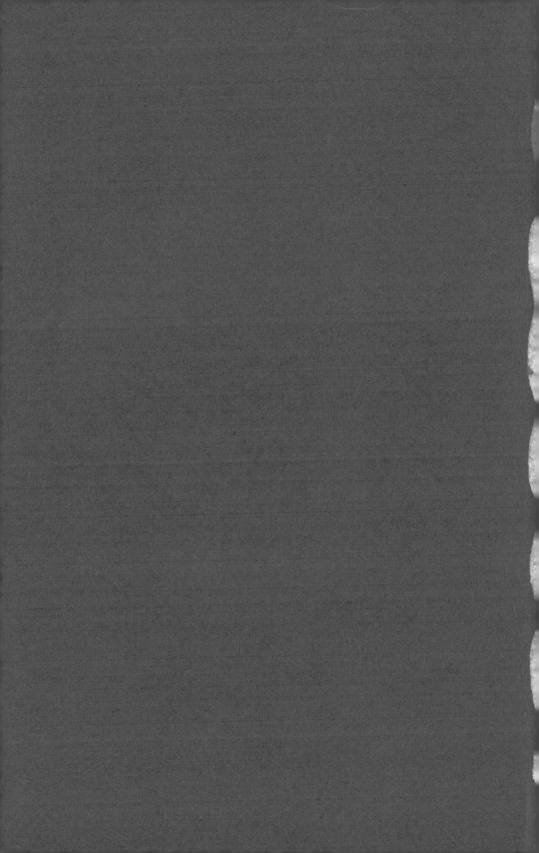

WOUNDED

Also by Percival Everett

Wounded

A Novel

PERCIVAL EVERETT

Graywolf Press
Saint Paul, Minnesota

Publication of this volume is made possible in part by a grant provided by the Minnesota State Arts Board, through an appropriation by the Minnesota State Legislature; a grant from the Wells Fargo Foundation Minnesota; and a grant from the National Endowment for the Arts, which believes that a great nation deserves great art. Significant support has also been provided by the Bush Foundation; Target, with support from the Target Foundation; the McKnight Foundation; and other generous contributions from foundations, corporations, and individuals. To these organizations and individuals we offer our heartfelt thanks.

MINNESOTA
STATE ARTS BOARD

NATIONAL
ENDOWMENT
FOR THE ARTS

Published by Graywolf Press
2402 University Avenue, Suite 203
Saint Paul, Minnesota 55114
All rights reserved.

www.graywolfpress.org

Published in the United States of America

ISBN 1-55597-427-9

2 4 6 8 9 7 5 3 1
First Graywolf Printing, 2005

Library of Congress Control Number: 2005925166

Cover design: Scott Sorenson

Cover photograph: Tim Flach © Getty Images

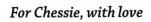

For Chessie, with love

WOUNDED

ONE

BY DEFINITION a cave must have an opening large enough to allow a human to enter. The cavity can be wind- or water-eroded. It can be miles and miles deep. But it must let a person enter. And that is what is scary about caves, that one can enter.

My heeler's ears cocked. I was holding the left hind hoof of my antsy mare. The bay kept leaning on me and swishing her tail in my face. She was a good horse, had good manners, but she was a little old and she got cranky when asked to hold up her foot for too long. I was rasping smooth a notch near her heel, trying to use long, efficient strokes, and wondering if I needed to put shoes on her. The break was nice and round and she had decent wall, so I wasn't too worried. I wasn't riding her much anyway, just a couple spins around the arena once a week to keep her in a semblance of good condition. My dog's ears perked again.

"Is that you, Wallace?" I asked. I didn't bother to look up. I continued to work, making another long rasp. I used my knife to whittle down to live hoof. I rubbed the smooth, white surface with my thumb.

"Yeah, it's me."

"You know, it's hard to sneak up on a man with a dog."

"I wasn't sneakin'."

I gave the hoof a last long look. "I guess not. Something wrong with the tractor, Wallace?"

"Why does something have to be wrong because I'm here?"

I let the horse's foot go and stood up straight, my bones cracking.

I considered that I felt like the horse and felt bad for having her hoof up for so long. My joints never used to complain like that, I thought. I watched the horse's foot settle back to the ground and gave her aging haunch a firm scratch. "You getting a little arthritic, old girl?" I asked her. Then, to the man, "Okay, what's the problem, Wallace?"

"Ain't no problem."

"Then, Wallace, why aren't you mowing the pasture?" I looked out the barn doors at the trees alongside the field.

"Takin' a break." Wallace shuffled his long feet, then stopped, his dusty boots together, pointing his toes straight ahead, awkwardly. "Thought I'd stop for a while."

"That's reasonable, Wallace. It's really hot out there. I was thinking about taking a break myself." I pushed my sleeves back up my arms, pulled out my kerchief and wiped my neck.

"Why don't you like me?" Wallace asked.

I looked up and down the barn alley. "Wallace, I'm afraid I'm having trouble following you, son."

"Why don't you like me?"

"Wallace, I like you fine. I hired you, didn't I?"

"That don't mean nothing."

I called my dog over and rubbed at her ears. Zoe groaned and leaned into the attention. "Wallace, I like you just dandy, okay? I don't want to go to town with you and dance and get drunk, but I like you."

"Very funny," Wallace said. "You're always making fun of me. How come you say my name every time you say something to me?"

"Wallace, it's your name. I didn't think you'd respond to Cisco or Fred."

"No, I mean every time you say something, you say my name. Every single time."

"Do I, Wallace?" I caught myself as I said it.

"See."

"I'm sorry, Wallace."

"What's that all about?"

"I'm sorry. I wasn't doing it on purpose." I blew out a breath and watched the man. He was tall, wiry, and what my father would have called a finger sandwich shy of a picnic.

Wallace shuffled in his tracks for a second time. "The mower blade broke," he said.

"Didn't I ask you if the tractor was okay, Wallace?"

"Yes, sir. The tractor's fine. Blade's broke. I guess I hit a big rock."

I reached down, picked up a bit of hoof trimming, and tossed it to Zoe. "Guess so. Didn't I tell you to walk that field first? Damn." I collected myself. "Well, Wallace," I emphasized saying his name, "things happen. At least you didn't whack off your leg or some other part. I'll take a look at it later. In the meantime, go on in the house and have Gus make you a sandwich."

"If you want I can try to weld the blade back on."

"No, no, no, that's okay, Wallace. You need lunch." The words felt too quick in my mouth and for a second I worried that I'd insulted the thin-skinned man again. "I'll take care of it. Go grab yourself some lunch."

I watched the man cross the corral, then walk through the yard to the back door of the house. He knocked on the screen door, perfunctorily, before entering. I thought Wallace was okay, a little dumb, but okay. I didn't know much about the man; I didn't care to know much. I'd hired him in spite of his obvious surprise at discovering I was black. He'd come to the house and stood on the porch for near five minutes without knocking. Gus looked out the window and shook his head, laughing. "That white boy is gonna stand out there till winter."

I opened the door and stepped out, asking what he wanted. He could barely get out that he was there about a job.

"My name is Wallace Castlebury."

"Okay," I said, trying to help him.

"I heard you need a ranch hand." He looked at his long feet, glancing up quickly to catch my eyes before looking away again.

"Yeah? Where'd you hear that?"

"At the feed store. The one in town," he stammered. "The woman who works there told me."

"You ever do ranch work before?"

"Some. Over near Shell."

"Who'd you work for?"

"Man named Fife. The Double R."

"I know him," I said. "Mind if I give him a call?"

The man shook his head. "You can call him."

I looked away from him toward the slope at the end of the large pasture. "Can you drive a tractor without killing yourself or others?"

"So far, sir." The sir came hard. "I've mowed and pulled a disc. I can work on them a little bit, too."

"Know anything about horses?" I asked.

"Which end kicks, that's all."

I think I smiled. "I reckon you'll do. You got a place to live?"

"Staying with a friend in town," Wallace said.

"Can you be here at seven in the morning? And I mean seven, not seven-thirty, not seven-fifteen. Every morning?"

Wallace said he could and I hired him. Then he stood on the porch, looking at his shoes, waiting.

"Wallace, you can go now. I'll see you in the morning at seven."

"Okay."

That had been our first meeting and for a month the subsequent encounters were not so different. Wallace wasn't completely inept, but he was as close as a man can get to it and still be alive. He did what I asked for the most part, not much more, thank god, and when he did show some inkling of initiative, his instincts nearly always turned out to be wrong. One time he used my ranch Jeep to pull the two-wheeled trailer I had filled with cut firewood to the back of the house. Once there he decided to uncouple the trailer. I watched him, not quite believing it. He, with almost complete focus, flipped the lever. Before I could shout out, the trailer seesawed back, throwing high the hitch and dumping the wood. He was lucky he didn't lose a finger, or more.

He stood there gawking at the spilled wood like that might clean it up. "Geez, I'm sorry, Mr. Hunt."

"That's okay, Wallace." I stepped around the mess. "Just empty the wood and stack it all here." I imagine that I was not successfully covering my expression of exasperation because he said, "I'm really sorry. I can reload it and put it wherever you want. That was stupid, weren't it?"

"Just stack it here, Wallace." I walked away a few strides, then turned back to him and said, "Wallace, yes it were."

The afternoon sun was burning into the west side of the barn where I was repairing a waterline. The white PVC was a great invention, but sunlight made it brittle. I'd sawn off the cracked section and was trying to couple in a new piece without covering my hands with the blue adhesive that I was certain would poison me somehow. The roof vents were spinning from the heat. I'd sent Wallace home early because of the broken mower blade and so he couldn't cause any more damage. The break in the blade wasn't bad, near the back, away from the cutting surface. I was glad for the quiet. I planned to weld the blade back on once the sun was down and the air had cooled some. I finished with the pipe, put my hacksaw, pipe pieces, and glue in the shade and walked through the barn, out and across the yard to the house. Gus was resting on the porch, sitting in a straight-backed chair.

"You forgot to eat lunch again." The old man lifted a hand and scratched his pathetic beard.

"If you shaved that thing off it wouldn't itch," I said. "And a man doesn't need lunch unless he remembers it."

"That's what you cowboys say, eh?" Gus said.

"That's what we say."

"Are you starving?" he asked.

"Now that you mention it." I looked off in the same direction as Gus. "Of course, there's a pot of elk chili simmering on the stove."

"No, but there's a salad in the icebox." Gus pulled out the pipe he never lit and bit down on it.

"Icebox? Who says icebox anymore?"

"I do. I'm an old man. I also say movie house and dang fool. Want to make something of it?"

"I think I'll bring my salad out here to eat. Want some?"

"No, thanks."

"It's a nice evening," he said. "Quiet."

"Very quiet."

The greenish sparrows under the eave of the little barn weren't crazy about the roar of the tractor so early and they liked even less the sparking and brightness of the arc welder. I'd forgotten about the blade and so I was up in the pre-dawn, in the cool air, sweating under the welding hood. I'd been careful to take off the mower blade and set it properly, but my seam, as usual, was pathetic. Gus always teased me, telling me I couldn't weld a straight dot. Zoe looked up from her spot some yards away, then I heard the truck. I lifted the mask and stood. A white, late-seventies Ford dually kicked up dust as it approached. I looked at my watch. The young woman driving skidded more than she'd intended when stopping. A skinny cowboy leaned an unshaven face out the passenger-side window.

"You John Hunt?" the man asked.

I nodded.

"Is Wallace here?"

"It's five-thirty in the morning, son." When the kid didn't say anything, I said, "No, he's not here. Would you like me to give him a message for you? I expect him at seven."

"Naw, ain't no message."

"Suit yourself."

The woman put the fat truck in gear and they drove away with a little more decorum.

Gus came out of the house in his robe and walked across the yard. "Who the Sam Hill was that?"

"Some kids looking for Wallace."

"It's five-thirty in the morning," Gus said.

"I pointed that out to them."

"Well, come on in and have some breakfast, stupid."

"Okay, captain."

Gus walked ahead of me. From behind him I studied his khakis and white T-shirt that was his uniform. The old man limped, favoring his left leg. But at seventy-nine, he was still strong and it showed in the way he moved, deliberately, always with conviction. Uncle Gus had spent eleven years in a state prison in Arizona for murder. He killed a man who was raping his wife. The fact that the man had been white was Gus's explanation for his time in prison. Gus would say that the reason you never saw any black people in the state of Arizona was because they were all in prison. But Gus was never bitter. He was hard, but never bitter. He'd come to live with me after Susie's death.

In my dream, I spoke to a mirror, telling myself that I was speaking windy nonsense. That was what I said. "You're speaking windy nonsense." Then, as if to stop the dream, I wondered whether the windy nonsense was, in fact, a complaint about the expression "windy nonsense." But then the talk to the mirror turned to the accident and all I could do was swear at myself, call myself stupid. And slow. "You're a selfish bastard," I said over and over, until there was no mirror, just another me and I didn't know which one to believe, even though they were saying the same thing.

I'd lost Susie during a dry spring. It was a hot May day. I'd been in town all morning picking up supplies. My foreman Tad met me as I drove up. He came to the truck's window, holding the de-worming chart.

"You got the stuff?" he asked, conspiratorially.

"Yeah, here it is." I handed over a case of de-worming paste from the passenger seat. "I really think we've got to put them on a split rotation. There're getting to be too many horses to do all at once."

"I'd have to agree with you," Tad said.

I looked past Tad to the short arena behind the house. My wife Susie was checking the cinch on the new Appaloosa. "Hey, Tad, what's my wife doing with the App?"

Tad looked back. "Don't know. Maybe she's going to lunge him."

"Well, okay," I said. I had an uneasy feeling. "I told her to let me work with that horse a few days before she got on him."

Tad starting telling me that one of the horses had wind puffs.

But I was noticing that Susie was holding a crop and not the lunging whip. "Tad, is she about to get on that horse?"

Tad looked again. "Looks like it."

I pulled myself out of the truck and started walking toward the arena. Things turned sour in a hurry. Once Susie's butt settled on the saddle the mare spun to the left and reared slightly. I broke out into a trot. I heard Susie shout "whoa!" to no obvious effect. I was running now and I could hear Tad's footfalls behind me. I called out to Susie. The horse reared again, this time higher. Susie fell head over hind end off the back of the horse. The horse kicked out and I thought I saw a hoof catch my wife's helmet as her light body spun just before hitting the ground. I took the fence in a bound and landed on my knees next to Susie's motionless body. There was dust, nothing but dust, so much dust I couldn't see her face, couldn't see where the horse had run. I choked on the dust, holding Susie and trying to find her.

After breakfast, and after finishing the blade, and feeding the horses and riding the new mare, I stood on the porch and looked at the sky. Gus joined me. "It's nine," I said, "and where's Wallace?"

"Probably tied one on last night."

"Well, I'm not waiting around for him. You ready to go?"

"Yeah, I'm ready. Whatever the hell that means."

"That means do you have on clean socks and undies?"

"As a matter of fact," he said.

"Well, let's go."

Gus grabbed his jacket and got into the Jeep. He drove out the drive toward the road. "I'll be damned if I'm paying him for today even if he shows up and works late," I said. I looked over at my uncle. "And don't forget to tell the doctor about your shortness of breath."

"Yes, Mother."

I followed the dirt road to the highway and turned toward town. I looked up at the mountains. There had been an early dusting of snow up high, but the valley was unseasonably hot. I was eagerly anticipating a free day to go and root around in the caves. I'd discovered them years earlier on the BLM land south of my ranch. I didn't know what I expected to find or learn in them, but I thought of them often.

We made the big curve and came over the hill and looked down on town. I was never quite prepared for the sight of it, though I'd lived outside it for twenty years. Even when it had been tiny, its abrupt appearance after the bend always made it seem large. Now, with a couple of housing developments and the new community college campus and the strip malls that followed, it was damn near urban sprawl.

"I don't know why you let this place bug you so much," Gus said. "It's just a town and not much of one. Just a bunch of buildings where people live and work. Hell, it's not like it's Phoenix."

"It was fine ten years ago." I glanced at the fuel gauge and made a note to fill up. "It used to be a village, a real Western town. Now, now it's working on being just like anyplace else."

"Get off your soapbox."

I shut up.

"Did you remember to bring the list?"

I felt my breast pocket and said I did. I was always forgetting lists. I was good at making them and, with the list in my pocket, I could take care of everything without looking at it. But my habit was to forget the list, and then I couldn't recall a damn thing. "Are you sure you don't want me to wait for you at the doctor's office?"

"I'm sure. When he's done poking me, I'll just want to grab a bite and head home."

I pulled into a diagonal space in front of the doctor's office and watched the old man walk through the door. I then drove to the opposite side of town, not far, to the Broken Horn Feed Store.

The doors of the store always sported some new, tacky novelty that the shop owner, Myra, hadn't been able to resist. Today it was a pony-sized, stuffed horse with eyes that followed anyone who walked by and said, "Clippity-clop, cowpoke" in a John Wayne voice. I watched the eyeballs track me to the counter, then reset.

"That's real nice, Myra," I said.

"Ain't it a hoot?"

"That's what it is, all right. What else does it do?" I asked.

"Well, it doesn't shit on the floor." Myra flashed her wide, gap-toothed smile. "Around here that's a pretty good trick."

"I reckon. Say, do you have my de-worming paste all packed up?"

"Not yet. I was in the middle of doing that now."

"That's fine," I said. "I've got a whole list of stuff. I'll get what I need while you wrap it up."

"How's that ancient uncle of yours?" she asked as I stepped away.

"He's at the doc's right now getting his oil checked," I said. "He's okay. He doesn't say much about how he feels."

I walked over to the wall of bits and bridles. I always marveled at the wide array of shapes, weights, and materials of the bits. Many were beautiful. All were meant to cause possible discomfort. Some were harsher than others and served as a reminder of how cruel people could be. I picked up a bicycle chain mule bit and felt a chill creep over me. The only positive thing was that this bit had remained on the wall unsold for at least five years. I put it back and went on to collect my Betadyne, drawing salve, and other things. I piled the stuff on the counter.

Myra came from the back with my box. "Hey, did you hear about that boy?"

"I don't think so. What boy?"

"They found this college kid dead at the mouth of Damon Falls Canyon." Myra shook her head. "I heard he was strung up like an elk with his throat slit."

"My god." I looked outside at the road. The image made my stomach turn a bit and I swallowed hard. A gasoline truck rumbled by. "My god," I said, again. "What the hell happened. Was he robbed?" I didn't know why I was asking that question. I imagined I was just trying to have a senseless thing make sense. I stared at Myra.

"I don't know. It's pretty awful, though. You know, people are just animals anymore."

"No, they're people. That's the problem. Did they catch who did it?"

Myra shook her head. "I haven't heard anything about that." She totaled up the bill.

I wrote out a check. I noticed my hand trembling a bit, then it stopped. "There you go, ma'am."

"You tell that uncle of yours I asked about him."

"I will, Myra."

I left the store, put my supplies in the back of the Jeep, then sat behind the wheel, staring through the glass at the empty bench on the deck by the front door. I glanced at my rearview mirror and caught sight of a flatbed loaded with hay pass by. I cranked the engine, backed out and pulled away; the crunching of the gravel gave me comfort.

At the Lone Steer, a diner that seemed to change ownership monthly but never changed, I sat near the end of the long counter and ordered coffee from a young woman who managed to tell me between my ordering and her delivering it that she was only there to earn enough money to go back to college in Fort Collins and that she would never marry another man from Wyoming, especially a cowboy, no matter how cute he or his horse was.

"Maybe you shouldn't marry a man at all," I said, more into my cup than right to her. "We're nothing but trouble."

Yeah," she agreed, nodded. "That's about the truest thing I ever heard a man say."

"Trouble's all I've ever given myself," I said.

"And that would be because you're no damn good." This from Duncan Camp who had straddled the stool next to me.

"I told them to put a screen on that door," I said.

"How you doin', buddy?" he asked.

"I'm okay. You?"

"I'm as fine as frog's hair," he said. "Hell, partner, if'n I was any finer, I'd be sick."

"That's pretty fine."

"Where's Unc?" Duncan asked.

"I'm meeting him for lunch in a few minutes. As he likes to put it, the doctor's got him on the rack right about now."

"You're not eating here?" Duncan whispered.

Whispering back, "No way. I'm trying to keep the old guy alive. Talk about wasting a trip to the doctor."

Duncan laughed. The waitress slid his coffee in front of him, and he took a sip. "You hear about that boy?"

"A few minutes ago."

"Awful, just awful, thing like that. The paper didn't say much, but I heard whoever did it stretched him out like Christ." Duncan caught the waitress's eye. "Darlin', are those doughnuts made here on the premises?"

"No, sir."

"Let me have one, then," he said.

"I heard the boy was gay," the waitress said.

"Well, I don't know anything about that," Duncan said. "But it's a damn shame any way you cut it. Bad choice of words."

"Any idea who did it?" I asked.

"Hell if I know," Duncan said. "All I know is I'm keeping my daughters close to the ranch for a while. You don't know what kind of weirdos are prowling around out there. Worse yet, we do know. Wolves ain't nothing compared to a sick person." Duncan shook his head and poured a generous amount of sugar into his coffee. "Can I get some milk over here, darlin'?"

"How are things at your place?" I asked.

"I had two horses come down with the strangles. God knows where it came from. And I'm struggling to get the hay in before it rains."

"Horses okay now?"

"Yeah, they're fine. By the way, horse trainer, I've got a horse I'd like you to work on for me."

I finished my coffee and set down my mug with a thud. "I'd expect you to pay me."

"Damn. All anybody can think about in this country is money. What about this poor horse that needs your sweet, loving attention?"

"What's the problem?" I asked.

"One thing, he's a horse. The other thing is the idiot's afraid of his own shadow. He bolts for no apparent reason. Usually with somebody on his back. Namely, me. I'm figuring that's a bad thing."

"There's always a reason," I said. "How old is the idiot?"

"Five, six. I'm not sure. I just bought him and I don't know much about his history. He's a beautiful animal." Duncan took a bite of his doughnut. "But he sees demons, this guy."

"Well, bring him over and leave him with me for a while. He does trailer?" I asked.

"Yeah."

The little bell on the front door rang and I turned to see if it was Gus entering the diner. It wasn't. It was the young deputy, Hanks. He caught sight of me and made his way to me.

"Oh lord, what'd you do now?" Duncan said and laughed.

"Mr. Hunt?" the deputy asked.

"What can I do for you, son?"

"The sheriff told me to find you and ask you to come over to his office. I called your place and then I drove out, but you weren't there."

"Why does Bucky want to see me?" I asked.

The deputy was nervous or excited. He thumbed the top edge of his thick black belt. "It's about a prisoner," he said.

"Prisoner?"

"That's all I can tell you."

I looked over at Duncan. Duncan shrugged and I said, "I guess I'd better go see what this is all about."

"I reckon," Duncan said.

"Tell Gus to wait for me here when he shows up."

Duncan nodded. "Will do. I'll wait till he gets here."

"Thanks."

The sheriff's name was Bucky Edmonds. He was a slow-moving but generally agreeable sort. He was extremely tall and so never seemed completely comfortable, never quite convincing when trying to be intimidating, and he always appeared a bit of a clown when caught indoors. Still, he was well meaning enough. When Hanks led me into the station the sheriff was hovering over the dispatcher near the front desk.

"You wanted me, Bucky?" I asked.

"I found him," Hanks said.

"I can see that, deputy." Then to me, "You know a fella named William Caitlinburg?"

I shook my head. "I don't believe I do."

"Says he works for you."

"Wallace Castlebury?"

Bucky shot a look at Hanks. "Damn your handwriting, Hanks." Edmond scratched the correction onto the form. "Wallace Castlebury," he repeated the name. "You do know him then."

"He's worked for me for almost four weeks now. Why?"

"I got him locked up back there." Edmonds tossed a thumb over his shoulder. "I haven't questioned him yet. Hanks here and Douglas talked to him and he asked for you."

"My first question, I guess, is 'what did he do?' and my second is 'why the hell are you telling me?'" I rubbed the back of my neck.

"Like I said, John, he asked for you. He says he doesn't know anybody else around here. You're his phone call, so to speak."

"He has some friends," I said.

"He asked for you."

"This idiot's not expecting me to go his bail, is he?" I asked. When the sheriff didn't answer, I said, "Is he, Bucky?"

"I doubt there's going to be any bail."

I studied the tall man's face.

"He's in here for murder. We're pretty sure he's the one who killed that boy last night."

"And what am I supposed to talk to him about?"

"He asked for you. That's all I can tell you. You're not obliged to talk to him. I take it he's not a friend of yours?"

"Has he been assigned a lawyer yet?" I asked.

"Not yet. We picked him up two hours ago. A defender's driving up from Laramie. I'm not talking to him until his counsel gets here." Edmonds pulled a pack of gum from his breast pocket and folded a stick into his mouth. "Want one?"

I shook my head. "I'll talk to him for a minute."

Edmonds whistled over to Hanks. "Deputy, I want you to walk Mr. Hunt back to the tank and let him talk to Castlebury." He put emphasis on "Castlebury."

I followed Hanks down a bright hallway and through a locked door that was less massive and impressive than I had imagined. Wallace was sitting on a metal cot behind a barred door.

"You've got a visitor," Hanks said, sounding official. Then to me, "Just knock when you're done."

"I won't be long," I told him, hoping that he would understand that I didn't want him wandering away. I watched the door close, then heard the lock catch. The sound gave me an unsteady feeling. I kept my distance from the cell door and looked at Wallce. He looked even more washed out than usual. His face was drawn, his eyes baggy. I was trying to wrap my thinking around the idea that he had killed someone. "You're in jail, Wallace," I said.

"They say I killed a guy," he said, coming to the bars. He sounded just like the Wallace I knew. He studied the bars and shivered as if feeling a draft. He held them for a second then let them go.

"That's what they're saying," I said.

"I didn't do it."

"I'm not your lawyer, son."

"I don't know nobody else."

"I thought you told me you were staying with a friend?"

He backed up and sat on the cot, looked at his hands folded in his lap. He shook his head.

"A boy and a girl came looking for you this morning. White dually."

He didn't say anything.

I started to turn away.

"I got a brother in Fort Collins. His name is Gary. My folks is dead. All I got is my brother. He hates me, though. He won't do nothing for me. He hates me, always has."

"What about the kids in the white dually?"

"I don't know who you're talking about."

"Listen, I'll try to reach your brother, Wallace," I said. I didn't want to say it. "I'll call him and tell what's happened. I'll give him what I owe you for the week. It won't be much, maybe he can use the money to help pay the lawyer or something. Hell, I don't know."

"You believe I didn't do it," Wallace said.

I looked at the stupid face. "I'm not even sure what they're saying you did. I don't know you, Wallace. You're not a friend of mine. Hell, you're barely an acquaintance. You're not even a good worker. Besides, it doesn't matter whether I believe you or not. You're in a world of trouble and that's what you need to be worried about. All the same, I'll try to reach your brother." I stepped away and knocked on the door.

Hanks opened it immediately. "You done?"

"Yeah, I'm done."

"Mr. Hunt," Wallace said. He was up now and at the door, gripping the bars in a pathetically clichéd way.

"Yes, Wallace?"

"I'm scared."

I nodded.

Bucky was still by the dispatcher when I came out. "Well?" he asked.

"Says he didn't do it, wants me to call his brother in Fort Collins. I think that's what he wants."

The horse isn't supposed to make decisions. That's the first thing. The second thing is that the rider *is* supposed to make decisions. If the horse gets ahead of you, you might get left behind. That's the old saying. So, you've got to redirect the animal, break the routine, ride him between some bushes for no apparent reason. Don't let him get chargey on steep hills.

TWO

AT THE FIRST SIGN of the green horse's nose going up, the trainer should put on a running martingale. If he lets the nose get up, it's too late to put the rings on.

The next day, I found myself faced with the unwelcome prospect of putting in a call to Wallace's brother. I didn't do it right away. I fed the horses, mucked out the stalls, and built a long-needed shelf in the tack room, nicking my finger in the process. Still, I'd said I would call and so I would. I put the tools back into the big red box, congratulated myself for doing so because I never put tools back where they belonged, and walked across the yard to the house. The air was still warm, but I could feel autumn coming. In the house, I settled behind the desk in my study and began cleaning my only rifle, an old Weatherby I'd had for years. I supposed in some way I liked the weight and feel of it, but I didn't much like guns. Cleaning it reminded me of my father, his insistence on a tidy rifle. He thought one should show respect for the danger and the necessity of the thing. I appreciated the danger part, but the necessity part had only presented itself once, when I found an injured moose up mountain and had to put the animal out of his misery; as the animal had dragged himself around a four-meter circle, I wondered whether I would be ending his pain or my own on seeing him. The moose looked at me as I drew a bead and, in my human way, I imagined his asking for release. I guess I believed that a dirty gun was a scary one. I was pausing to inhale the scent of the gun oil when Gus plunked the phone down in front of me.

"What's that for?" I asked.

"The only time you clean that damned rifle, that you don't use, is when you're procrastinating."

"If that were true, this would be the cleanest gun in the West."

Gus turned and left the room.

I picked up the phone and called information in Fort Collins. I asked for a Gary Castlebury; how many Castleburys could there be? There were in fact two G. A. Castleburys. I took both numbers and, of course, the first one I dialed was wrong. I dialed the second. A man answered.

"May I speak to Gary Castlebury?"

Silence on the other end.

"Hello?" I looked out the window at some gathering clouds.

"Who's this?" the man asked.

"I'm trying to reach Wallace Castlebury's brother," I said. "Are you Gary?"

"What do you want?"

"Are you Gary Castlebury?"

"What do you want?"

"My name is John Hunt. Your brother worked for me for a couple of weeks."

"So?" I felt that the man was about to hang up.

"Your brother asked me to get in touch with you. He's gotten himself into some trouble up here in Highland. Actually, he's in a lot of trouble."

"What's that supposed to mean to me?" the man said. "Quite a lot of trouble."

"Wallace is your brother, isn't he?" I asked.

"What kind of fuckin' trouble is the asshole in now?"

"He's been arrested for murder."

Gary Castlebury was silent for a few seconds. Then he snorted, sounding almost like he was laughing. "That son of a bitch is too lazy to kill anybody."

I didn't say anything.

"What's he want from me?" he asked.

"I told him I'd call you."

"Well, thanks for callin'. You have a nice day now," he said and with that he was off the phone.

I looked at the dead receiver and placed it back onto the cradle.

Gus had come to the doorway. "So?" he asked.

"That boy's floating on a river of lava in a rubber raft." I stood and locked my rifle back in the cabinet. "But you know what?"

"What?"

"It's none of my business."

Duncan Camp drove into my place with his single-horse trailer in tow behind his pickup. The trailer was open topped, a white affair with a broad green stripe, and in it stood a truly monstrous palomino.

"What the hell is that?" I asked as Duncan pulled himself out of his truck.

"It's a horse, John," Duncan said. "I'm surprised at you. Equus caballum."

"Caballus," I said.

"That's what I said."

"A horse. You sure?" I asked.

"Pretty sure," Duncan said. "He's got a horse brain, I can tell you that."

"You want him for riding or picking apples?"

Duncan coughed into his fist, then took out a cigarette. "He's a big one, all right." He lit up. "Fifteen hundred pounds of dumb muscle and bad attitude." He looked at the burning cigarette in his hand. "Doctor said these things are going to kill me. But he didn't say when. I can't work with imprecise information."

"So, he spooks," I said.

"Did I mention that he's hard to catch?"

"Not until now," I said. "He trailers okay, though." It was more a question than an observation.

"He has his moments."

"My daughter named him Felony."

"That's charming." I looked at the horse's eyes. Felony looked frightened and he was snorting and prancing in place. "We'd better get him out of there. I want you to stick him in the round pen. Take off his halter."

Duncan backed the horse out of the trailer; the animal swung his hindquarters around sharply before he was clear of the ramp. The big man lost his balance, but he didn't fall.

"You okay?" I asked.

"Yeah, I'm just getting old." Duncan turned the horse and walked him toward the round pen. "You gonna start with him now?"

"Might as well see what I'm getting myself into," I said.

Duncan walked the horse into the pen, removed the halter as I had instructed, and came back out. He stepped onto the observation deck with me, and we watched the animal trot and canter around the circle, one way and then the other.

"He's a pretty mover," I said. "Big cus."

Duncan didn't say anything.

"What's he do when you try to catch him?" I asked.

"You might say he can be a little chargey," Duncan said.

I laughed and looked Duncan in the eye. "How chargey?"

"Oh, he'll come right at you sometimes. Mostly, though, he just gives you his butt."

"How hard?" I asked. "When he comes right at you?"

"Varies," he said.

"So, he spooks under saddle and attacks when he's not." I took Duncan's silence as agreement. I said, "I say we shoot him."

"He sure is pretty," Duncan said.

"Okay, we shoot him and stuff him." I blew out a breath. "Well, I guess it's time to see what we've got in there. Let me have the halter and lead rope."

Duncan handed them to me. "What do you want me to do?" he asked.

"Call nine-one-one."

I climbed down the steps and walked into the pen, holding the halter in my right hand and I held the tail end of the cotton lead rope in my left. The other end was still fastened to the halter. The horse pulled up on seeing me and sped away in the opposite direction. He kicked up more dust and when I was in the center of the circle, the horse started storming clockwise around me. I picked a spot on the wall opposite the gate. When the horse approached that spot, I tossed the halter out, hanging on to the end of the rope. Felony put on the brakes, rolled back, and tore off anti-clockwise. When the animal came to the same point on the circle, I tossed out the halter again. This time the horse paused and trotted by it. I talked to the horse the whole time, calling his name, making soothing sounds.

"You okay?" Duncan asked.

"Yep."

Every time the horse came to that spot, I tossed the halter. Soon the horse was slowing when approaching the spot. After a couple more tosses, he was stopping at the spot and turning to face me. That was what I wanted. I then pushed the horse away with a large gesture of my arms. When he stopped again, I turned my back to him and took a step away. Felony followed me across the pen. I turned and let the horse sniff the halter. He let me stroke his neck. I left the pen.

"That was great," Duncan said, coming down from the platform.

"I can work with him," I said. "Is there anything you know that he's particularly afraid of?"

"John, he's scared of everything. A squirrel spooked him. Once he caught sight of his reflection in a truck window and took off. Who knows? All I know is I don't have many wrecks left in me at my age."

"Well, I'll work with him for a few weeks."

Duncan looked at his watch. "I'm late. Hell, I'm always late. I didn't expect you to start right away."

"I'll give you a call when I know more," I said. We started walking back to his truck. "Are you going to be the one riding him?"

"Mostly," Duncan said. "Unfortunately, my daughter's in love with him. She'll want to ride him. I would like to put other people on him."

"We'll see," I said. "We might have to have Ginny come over and ride him here some."

"She'll like that," he said.

Duncan opened his truck door. "That was great."

"Well, we'll see how it goes," I said.

In my dream, I was working a string of seven green horses. It was too many and I knew it. I didn't have enough time to train them correctly. Every horse bucked and I found myself resorting to popping the animal I was riding with a quirt. Every time the horse bucked, I'd reach out and whip him on the snoot. But he wouldn't stop bucking and when I looked over at the hitching post I saw the other six horses, saddled, tied, waiting and bucking in place.

All day long woolly, white clouds had clumped together over the mountains and I expected rain, so I worked like mad trying to get my hay in. But there would be no rain that night. The clouds had already rolled past and so I left off with the last of the hay and saddled my Appaloosa. I packed a canteen and a little food and rode out the south gate and toward the creek. I had to admit to myself that I was bothered by my failure with Wallace's brother, but I had only said I would call, not that I would get him to come. I was also bothered by my decided lack of interest in Wallace Castlebury's predicament. I am by nature loyal and it felt bad simply to abandon the man, despite his brief presence on the ranch and despite the fact that I found the man generally objectionable. I didn't know if Wallace was guilty or not and I didn't care. He was nothing to me. I wasn't his lawyer or a cop. I'd made the call and that was it. I hoped the ride would clear my head. Zoe trotted some yards ahead of me and darted off after the occasional rabbit.

The creek was late summer low, a couple yards wide. The Appy crossed it without hesitation, which was unusual, and I took it as a good sign. I had an hour of light left and so I decided to ride all the way to the mouth of the cave and ride back in the dark. I'd discovered the cave several years into living in the area. I happened on it while chasing down a cagey bull back when I ran cattle. The cave was deep enough that I didn't know how deep it was. Susie and I had taken picnics and camped there regularly for a while. She'd never liked it.

"I don't want to go any farther," Susie said.

I turned to her. She was backlit by the entrance to the cave. Still, I could see the fear, if not on her face then by her posture. A chipmunk had found the picnic we'd set up some yards outside the cave.

"I don't like it in here," she said.

I pointed the beam of my flashlight into the darkness, showing a twist of passage. I realized that once we made that turn, the outside light would be lost and Susie would really become frightened. "You go on back, I'm going to look a little deeper," I said.

"No." She shook her hands at her sides. "This makes me so nervous." Her voice broke. "I'm scared."

I went back to her. "I'm sorry, Susie. Come on, let's go back and have some fruit. If that chipmunk left us anything."

"I don't mean to be such a baby," she said.

We walked out and Susie sat cross-legged on the blanket.

"If it scares you, it scares you. That's pretty simple. There's absolutely nothing to apologize about." I sat and leaned back against a large rock. "I can come back here some other time."

"I don't want you to," she said. "Just the idea of your being in here terrifies me. Really, I'm not making it up."

"Okay, honey."

Susie stood. She trembled as she looked down the slope then out over the Red Desert.

I got up and put my arms around her. "Everything's okay," I told her. "Everything is just fine."

"No, it's not," she said. "Can we go back to the house now?"

"You bet."

"I'm sorry, John."

"Don't be silly," I said. "We'll go back home. What's the big deal? Come on, let's pack up."

Zoe was back from chasing a rabbit, heeling to the App. I had sneaked back to the cave many times while Susie was alive. She must have known, but she never said anything. I stopped going shortly before her death, feeling that somehow I was cheating on her by being in the cave.

The sun was gone by the time I reached the entrance. I still hadn't been back in. But I wanted to explore it. I got off and looked into the dark mouth while my horse rested. Then I mounted and started back.

It was good and dark when I loosened the horse's cinch and walked him the last hundred yards to the hitching post beneath the flickering vapor lamp on the barn. A hatch of white flies darted in and out of the glow well above me. I took off the saddle and took my time brushing the horse. I had started cleaning out a hoof when I noticed a car parked in front of the house. It was a light-colored convertible, seemingly new, that I didn't recognize. I cleaned all the hooves, led the horse to her stall, and walked to the house. My body felt creaky.

"Who goes there?" Gus called as I stepped into the kitchen.

"Who does the fancy chariot belong to?" I asked.

"That would be mine." It was Morgan Reese from the neighboring ranch. She was a frequent visitor.

"Hey there, Morgan," I said. "What's up with the new wheels?"

"I got sick of driving a truck to Billings," she said.

"How much will it tow?" I asked.

"Who cares," she said, "it's a guy magnet. So where were you? Scaring cougars or kissing elk?"

"A little of both." I moved to take a seat at the table across from her, but I remembered and felt how dirty I was. "Are you going to stick around and have some dinner with us?"

"Gus already asked and I said 'you bet.'"

"Well. If you two will excuse me, I'll go upstairs and try to get cleaned up. It's one thing to come in after a ride and settle down to chow with a scraggly old geezer, but it's something else to sit down to a meal with a spiffy cowgirl who drives up in a white convertible."

I walked up the stairs, undressed, and left my clothes on the bathroom floor. I stepped into the shower and found myself thinking about Morgan. She was around a lot. I wasn't stupid or blind and so I knew she had a crush on me. I didn't mind her presence, in fact, it was sort of nice, and I tried to rationalize that by recognizing her as a good friend for Gus. Susie had been dead for six years and I know that most people would have moved on in that time, but I couldn't seem to. I missed my wife and I knew that wouldn't go away; I honestly didn't want that feeling to pass. But I had trouble imagining myself close to anyone again. My clumsiness around Morgan made me feel tense, uneasy, and my defense was to step away and the step away made me feel bad and so I felt more awkward still. While I dried, staring at my face in the mirror, I was amused by my all too apparent observation that I wasn't getting any younger.

"Hey, Hunt!" Morgan called up the stairs.

"What do you want?"

"Get your fanny down here!"

"I'm coming. Just let me put some pants on." I pulled on a clean pair of khakis and a white shirt and walked down the stairs and into the kitchen.

"You clean up real nice," Morgan said.

"Thank you ma'am," I said.

Gus shook his head over by the sink. "Don't lie to the poor bastard. He'll start to believe it, then he'll think he can stop trying."

"What's to eat?" I asked.

"Meat and taters," Gus said. "And a leek, watercress, and endive salad."

I sat down at the table with Morgan. "You've been reading the magazines at the doctor's office again."

"What if I have?" he said. "Anyway, this just happened to be one of my favorites when I was in prison."

Morgan laughed.

Gus was not shy about the fact that he'd been locked away for a while. He didn't broadcast the information, but he never hid it.

Morgan drank from her water glass. "That Castlebury is going to get more than prison."

Gus put the rest of the food on the table and sat down.

"I guess somebody saw him kill that boy," Morgan said. "That's what I heard anyway."

"What else did you hear?" Gus asked.

I took some potatoes from the dish.

Gus gestured toward me with his fork. "Mr. Above-It-All over there thinks it's none of our business."

"It is now," Morgan said. "The boy he killed was gay and the word is Castlebury got mad when he made a pass at him. We're in the news because of all this. It's awful. Imagine that poor boy."

Gus whistled. "It's a terrible thing, killing somebody." Gus was quiet and we gave the moment its head.

Morgan looked at me. "Hunt, how would you feel if a man made a pass at you? Would it get you upset?"

"Never thought about it."

"Well, think about it," she said.

"I guess I ought to be flattered," I said, shrugging.

"What would you say?"

"I don't know," I said. "I guess I'd say the same thing I'd say to a woman who made a pass at me. 'No, thank you.'"

Morgan tore some bread from the loaf and put it on her plate. Gus cut me a hard look.

I hadn't meant to shut any gates, but damn if I hadn't by accident. "I forgot the wine," I said. "Can't have dinner without wine." I got up and went to the small rack across the kitchen. "Now, I think a nice Syrah would wash down a size-twelve roper just splendidly."

Morgan softened somewhat. "Okay, cowboy, that's what you'd say. How would you feel?"

I stood at the table, twisting the corkscrew. "I don't know, to tell the truth. It's never happened. I don't know any homosexuals. Well, if I do, I don't know that they are. Hell, I don't know if half the people I know are heterosexual. I don't want to know." I pulled out the cork. "Anyway, to answer your question: I don't know. Like I said, I guess I should feel flattered."

"I knew some in prison," Gus said. "They scared me."

"Gus," Morgan complained.

"Hell, Morgan, everybody scared me in prison. Besides, that was a different thing anyway. That raping and stuff that happens in the lockup, that's not sex or love, that's fighting. It's all about power, all that macho stuff. Well, anyway, that's how it seemed to me."

"Speaking of macho," I said, "how's your mother?"

"We're burying the battle-ax on Wednesday," she said, sipping her wine. "She's alive and all. I just don't know what else to do with her."

"Bury me next," Gus said.

"You expect me to dig a hole in this heat?" I said. "Think again."

"Mother's fine," Morgan said. "She's as wild as ever. I was going to bring her tonight, but wrestling is on television. You know, she's seventy and she still rides that crazy horse."

"What's his name?" I asked.

"Crazy Horse."

"Oh, yeah. How old is he?" I asked.

"Thirty-six," she said. "Can you believe that?"

I loved it. "That's great. Senior food and what kind of hay?"

"Alfalfa and timothy. It's expensive, but she doesn't eat all that much. Everybody else gets straight alfalfa." Morgan paused and studied me. "Gus, you ever notice how comfortable this man gets when the subject is horses?"

"Now that you mention it," Gus said.

"What's that supposed to mean?" I asked.

"Watch this," Morgan said. "Hey, Hunt. Women." She stared at me while she said it.

Gus laughed.

"What?" I put a bit of antelope steak in my mouth. "What?"

"Sex," Morgan said.

"Very funny," I said. I didn't know where to look. I drank some wine, sat back and crossed my legs.

"Look at him," Morgan said. "He's tenser than a Republican with a thought of his own."

I looked at Morgan, frowning a smile. "Where'd that come from?"

"Been waiting to use it."

"It's true, though," Morgan said.

"Anyway, Duncan Camp dropped off his extremely large, insane, and might I add, dangerous horse today."

Morgan threw up her hands. "He's a lost cause."

The next day, I drove into town to pick up some medicine for Gus. I stopped at the sheriff's office. There was a buzz in the street and I could feel it more than see or hear it. Three deputy rigs were diagonally parked on the street instead of the usual one. I walked up the steps and inside.

Bucky spotted me as I entered. "John."

"Bucky." I looked back out the window at the street. "Bucky, what's going on around here?"

"Seems we're national news. Seems we got ourselves a hate crime. Well, ain't they all?" Bucky moved his unlit cigar around in his mouth.

"I just wanted to come by and let Castlebury know I talked to his brother like he asked." I looked at the hallway that led back to the cells. "You can tell him for me. You can tell him, too, that his brother isn't coming."

"This guy anything to you?"

I shook my head. "No. I was going to end up firing him anyway. He's not too swift. You've probably noticed."

"He doesn't hide it well," Bucky said. "Tell me, what time did he leave your place on Thursday night?"

"I sent him home early, right after lunch. He screwed up the mower blade." I looked around at the unusual number of deputies in the office. "Are you expecting trouble, sheriff?" I asked in my best cowboy voice.

"Give me a break," Bucky said. "Hell, I don't know." He pulled his cigar out of his mouth and rubbed his face.

"So, Wallace did it for sure, eh?" I asked.

"There's an awful lot of physical evidence."

"If he did it, then he'll get what's coming to him, I guess." I felt stupid saying those words.

"Yeah," Bucky said.

"You'll give him the message, then," I said and turned to leave.

"I think you should tell him." Bucky put back his cigar. "He could claim I never delivered it."

"You know I don't want to have anything to do with this guy or any of this. If he killed the kid, then I have no sympathy." I sighed out a long breath, asking myself: what if he wasn't guilty? Would I have any sympathy for him then?

Bucky said, "Just give him the message and walk out."

A different deputy took me back to the cell this time. I told him just like I'd told Hanks, I would only be a second.

"Hey, Mister Hunt," Wallace said. He didn't get up from the cot this time, but just lay there.

"I called your brother," I said.

"Thanks."

"Don't thank me. I didn't make much of an impression on him. That's the fancy way of saying he's not coming to help you." I looked at the deputy who was looking at his own shoes.

"Thanks, anyway," Wallace said.

I nodded. I turned and stepped toward the deputy and the door.

"Mister Hunt," Wallace said.

I looked back at him. He was sitting up now, but still on the cot. He gripped the edge with his hands.

"I didn't kill that guy."

"Okay."

"I didn't kill him."

"All right, Wallace. You tell that to your lawyer."

"Don't you want to know why I didn't kill him?" Wallace lay back down and stared at the ceiling.

"Okay, I'll bite," I said.

"I'll wait outside," the deputy said.

"No," I said. But, of course, the young man was correct.

"I'll be right on the other side of the door. Just knock." He walked out. The door closed with that awful click.

"Okay, kid," I said. "Why?"

"I don't really know," he said.

"Jesus."

"I mean, I know, but—" he stopped. "Mister Hunt, I liked him. I really liked him. You know what I mean? Why would I have killed him?"

I shook my head. "I don't know, son."

He closed his eyes and seemed to be crying.

"I'm sorry, Wallace. I just came to tell you about your brother." I stepped over and tapped on the door. The deputy let me out.

THREE

I TOLD MYSELF, and therefore it was no doubt true, that I was not much impressed by Wallace Castlebury's predicament. By my reckoning, killing another person made someone a bad man. I frankly didn't believe that Wallace was innocent. And the law, though it seldom worked as advertised, was going to do for him what it could, probably a little more than it would have for me and a little less than it would have for Duncan Camp. That simply was the way it was, I told myself and reminded myself that I simply did not care.

The day had turned hot and the street felt like steaming food. I ducked into the library where it was air-conditioned. It was a routine stop once a week to read newspapers and magazines. I was able to at once counteract my chosen isolation and justify that choice. I read about the gay killing in the *Denver Post,* the *Washington Post,* the *St. Louis Times Dispatch,* and the *New York Times.* They all said about the same thing, with the Eastern papers offering the implication, if not outright accusation, that the crime was symptomatic of some rural or Western disease of intolerance. I thought, yes, it's called America. I wondered why the reported rash of fifty rapes in Central Park was not considered a similar indicator of regional moral breakdown. I saw the dead boy's name and it stuck with me for the first time and I felt a little ashamed by that. Jerry Tuttle. By all reports he was a small man, a gentle man, and like most murdered people, not deserving of what had happened to him.

"Mr. Hunt?" It was the librarian, Kent Hollis.

I looked up at his craggy face. "Mr. Hollis?"

"Would you like some coffee?" he asked. "I just made some."

I had seen Hollis and said hello many times, sometimes on the street when Hollis took lunchtime walks with his wheelchair-bound wife. She was a big woman with a loud, good nature, but Hollis was quiet. I always noticed his delicate hands.

"French roast," he said.

"No, thank you, Mr. Hollis." I had always called the man Mr. Hollis because he always called me Mr. Hunt. I called to him as he stepped away. "Mr. Hollis."

"Sir?"

"How long have I known you?" I asked.

"I don't know," he said. "Years. Many years."

"My name is John. I'd like you to call me John." I stood from the straight-backed chair and put my hand out. "You don't mind, do you?"

Hollis took my hand and shook. "Kent," he said.

"Kent," I repeated his name. "How is your wife?"

"She's fine."

"Glad to hear it."

"Coffee?" he offered again.

"No, thank you. I'd better get back to my place before it falls down. I find I can't get things done unless I do them."

Hollis laughed.

"See you next week" I said. I left, considering the man and his devotion to his wife. I imagined that if Susie had lived, I'd be caring for her the same way.

I was out riding with Morgan. I held up on the far bank of the creek and waited while she coaxed her horse, Square, through the rivulet. She reined the horse left down the bank and turned through the water and up the opposite side. I liked the way she sat her horse.

"Why'd you name that animal Square?" I asked.

"He just never fit in with the other horses," she said. "He's too sweet. He lets them run all over him."

"I'm not going to mention how tacky it is that you ride a Morgan horse."

"I admire the restraint," she said.

When we were higher, we let the horses go for a stretch, opening up into a lope across the big meadow. The air was cooler up there and it felt good on my face. The breeze pressed the ochre grasses down and the ground appeared to move in a gentle wave. We stopped at the edge of the meadow and studied the valley below. My house and barns were small in the distance. The Red Desert was far off to the left; I could just see the desolate edge of it.

"Don't you just love it?" I said. "This has got to be the most beautiful place in the world. Just think, somewhere out there in that godforsaken desert are wild horses kicking up dust."

"Dying of thirst and starving to death," Morgan said.

"Wet blanket."

We stepped on toward a higher spot.

"You ever going to run cattle again?" she asked.

"Probably not," I said.

"Why?"

"I don't like cows." I shifted my weight in the saddle. "Mainly, I don't like the businesses I had to sell cows to. Hell, I don't even eat much beef anymore."

"I like cows," Morgan said. "They've got kind eyes."

"Yeah, well."

"Do you like my eyes, Hunt?" she asked.

"What, you think you've got cow eyes?"

"Do you?" she asked again.

"If I say they're kind and gentle, that kinda makes them cow eyes," I said. I didn't know which way I was running.

"Do you?"

"Sure, I like your eyes, Morgan." I pushed back my hat and looked at her eyes. "What's this all about?"

"You know, I like Gus a lot," she said, "but Gus is not the reason I spend so much time at your place." She was looking into my eyes. "I like your eyes, John. I like them a lot."

I could see she was near panic. "I guess I know that," I said.

"Well?" she asked.

"Well, what?"

"Am I wasting my time?"

"What do you want from me?" I asked. "I'm your friend, right?"

Some jays screeched in a nearby pine.

"You're my friend," Morgan said. It was resignation. She dismounted, dropped her reins, and walked a few yards away.

I threw my right leg over the horn and slid off the saddle. "Morgan," I said, slowly moving to her. I put my hands on her shoulders and turned her around. She felt soft just then and uncharacteristically frail. "It took a lot of courage for you to say that, I know."

"Well, whoop-tee-do. Pin a medal on my underappreciated breast and let's see who salutes."

"Listen, I'm really very attracted to you," I told her. "I am, Morgan. But, and I know you don't want to hear this—but, I keep thinking about things."

"Susie's dead, Hunt."

"Well, that's it. I blame myself." I didn't want to talk about my dead wife, but had to once the topic surfaced. I realized I had more than one reason to talk about her. I needed to work through it all myself. "Susie was afraid of a lot of things," I said. "You wouldn't know anything about that. I didn't understand and I'm not sure I really know now what it was like for her. It made her real negative about stuff and I guess her negativity started to make me irritable."

"Hunt."

"Let me finish," I said. "Susie would say something and I'd feel myself start to shut down. I'm sure she saw it. She was smart. I believe she began to think I didn't like her." I sat on the ground and stared at my house, at the corral where Susie had been killed. Morgan sat beside me. "I honestly think she was trying that horse so I would see her as brave."

"That's crazy," Morgan said.

"Maybe," I said. "All I know is I hated the way I'd cringe when she said anything for a while. I would anticipate the complaint or the fear. Made me feel like shit. I started not liking myself. I reckon I'm still not too fond of me. Anyway, Morgan, I really appreciate the way you just spoke up."

"Appreciation noted."

I looked north at the clouds holding steady over the mountains.

"What do you say we ride back?" Morgan said.

We did, loping again across the meadow. We led the horses with loosened girths the last quarter-mile. The air was feeling a little more humid and I could smell the hay. At the barn, we tied up the horses and took off the bridles and saddles. Morgan and I reached for the same hoof pick.

She snatched it away and said, "Hey, cowboy, get your own."

We were standing close to each other. Before the moment became deadly and irrevocably awkward, I leaned forward and kissed her on the lips.

A rustling at the edge of the barn gave us a start. Then we saw Gus walking back toward the house. He said, without looking back, "About goddamn time."

I got in some more of my hay the next morning. I was covered with dust and my dust mask was still hanging around my neck. I sat on the edge of the water trough beside the house and rested. I took off my shirt, turned around and splashed myself with the water. I sat back down and closed my eyes. I must have drifted off because I suddenly felt Gus standing next to me.

"You're awfully quiet for an old man," I said, my eyes still closed.

"Learned it from my grandfather," Gus said. "He was a full-blooded Seminole Indian."

"So, you've told me." The phone rang inside. I opened my eyes and looked at Gus. "I suppose I'm going to answer that," I said.

Gus nodded. "It's for you. I can feel it."

"You can feel it, eh?"

"In my bones."

I groaned as I pushed myself to my feet. I walked up the steps and into the kitchen where I picked up the wall phone.

"John?"

"Yes?"

"It's Howard." Howard Thayer was a friend from college, the only one I'd managed to keep. We hadn't been in touch for over a year.

"Hey, poke," I said. "How are you?"

"I'm fine. You ranching it up out there?"

"You bet. How are Sylvia and the kids?" The heat of the sun through the window was making me perspire again. I grabbed a towel from the counter and wiped my neck. It was damp and felt good.

"Actually, I'm calling about one of the kids," Howard said. "David."

I untangled the cord and pulled the phone over to the table and sat. "Is he all right?"

"He's fine."

"How old is he now?"

"He's twenty," Howard said.

"God, that means you're old."

"Tell me about it," he said. "Hey, Davey's going to be up in Highland and I was wondering if you could look in on him. Take him to lunch or something. Just so he has a friend, you know."

"Of course. What's he doing up here?"

Howard paused briefly as if doing something away from the phone. "I don't know exactly. He'll be staying at the Rusty Spur Motel. Is that place okay? Is it a fleabag?"

"Yes, but it's a quaint fleabag."

"He arrives there on Friday," Howard said. "Driving out with a friend. So, what's it like out there?"

"Beautiful. Always beautiful," I told him. "How's Chicago?"

"Crowded, dirty, disgusting," he said. "It's hot and ready to turn cold. You should visit."

"So, David is twenty," I said. "Last time I saw him he was fifteen, I think."

"Yeah, fifteen. He's grown up some."

"Any possibility of you and Sylvia making it up here?"

"I don't think so," Howard said. "John, Sylvia and I split up. We're divorced now."

"That's too bad," I said, not knowing if I thought that or not. "Are you all right?"

"Everybody's okay," he said. "These things happen. What can I say? Listen, I'd better run. Thanks for looking in on my boy."

"Sure thing."

"Talk later," Howard said.

"Bye." I hung up.

Gus came in and snatched the damp towel off my shoulder. "What are you, some kind of heathen? I'll bet you were going to put that right back on the counter, weren't you?"

"I hadn't thought that far," I confessed.

"Well, of course you hadn't. Heathen." He sighed. "Who was that on the telling phone?"

"My friend Howard. You remember him. I went to college with him. His kid's going to be in town this weekend."

"Are you hungry?" Gus tossed the soiled towel onto the big pile in the laundry room.

"Not yet. I've got some more work to do."

I went out to the barns and checked all the animals. I probed around the corners and between the stacks of bales of hay trying to flush out any late-season rattlesnakes. Then I made sure the extra chain was fastened onto the paddock gate where I kept Daniel White Buffalo's mule. The damn thing was an escape artist. Fortunately, he hung around and never did anything more than nibble at the hay and visit the other horses and get them agitated.

I went back into the house and told Gus I didn't need dinner.

"That's fine with me," he said.

"I'm going to ride up and camp in the cave."

"You're an odd fellow, John Hunt."

"See you in the morning."

I saddled the Appy and rode out. Zoe went with me. Gus didn't mind not cooking. He was always happy with just cereal.

At the cave, I unrolled my bag and got a fire going. I cooked a couple of hot dogs, tossing a couple pieces on top of Zoe's dry food. "I don't know," I said to her, "this might make you a cannibal, a dog eating a hot dog."

Zoe didn't laugh.

The fire threw light and my shadow against the wall.

I put on my headlamp and walked deeper into the cave. Zoe was good to have along because I trusted her to be able to find her way out, even if I couldn't. Still, I used light sticks every thirty yards or so and at every bend. I had a sack of thirty. I didn't plan to go exploring deep into the unknown parts, only to visit the big cavern. The room was big relative to the rest of the cave, about the size of a small church, not that I had had much experience with churches. It was nothing like the big caverns at Carlsbad or the ones I'd seen in photographs. It was perhaps forty by forty feet with a ceiling of thirty at its highest point. Zoe stayed close by my leg and that was fine with me. My lantern didn't throw a lot of light and my headlamp threw less and only where I looked. Giant stalactites hung from the ceiling and stalagmites popped up from the floor, various shapes, sizes, and colors, yellow to red, some ghostly white. I sat and turned off my lights, keeping a hand on Zoe. The only light then was the green glow of the stick I'd broken and left near the entrance to the room. I tried not to touch the stalagmites near me. I'd read how people could damage the surfaces with oils from their skin. I listened to the quiet, interrupted only by the steady, random drips, the drips that came from the mountain above and left infinitesimal amounts of calcium carbonate to make and lengthen the stalactites. I decided I was a trogloxene, a creature that lives outside the cave, but returns frequently. I'd seen sign of small mammals near the entrance on occasion, but never deep within. I'd seen a couple of daddy longlegs, and knew there were probably other spiders. And there had to be something the spiders were eating. I imagined that there were some blind, colorless insects roaming about, but I wasn't educated enough to find them.

What I liked about the cave, and perhaps any cave, the idea of a cave, was the place where light from the outside ceased to have any influence. That was why I liked being in it at night. I turned my lamps back on and made my way back long before any of my light sticks might begin to fade.

Back at my bedroll, I put a couple of medium-sized sticks on the embers and gave them a gentle blow until they showed orange and flared. I then added the split end of a fat log I'd dragged in earlier. Zoe trotted off outside to take care of business and I followed.

I started back to my house well before first light. I couldn't sleep because of Zoe's snoring and for some reason my horse would not stand easy at the cave's mouth. As I made my way across the creek and through the south gate, I thought something looked odd near the barn. As I reached the edge of the big field I couldn't believe what I was seeing. The mule was lying on his side, trying to wriggle his body under the bottom rail of the paddock fence. I rode up slowly and looked down at him. Only his head and neck were out, but they were well out. The mule opened his right eye wide and looked up at me, but, in that mule way, he didn't panic. He just let his head slap into the dust and lay there.

"So, what now?" I asked in a calm voice.

The mule didn't move.

I dismounted and dropped to my knee in front of the animal's nose. This was a potential disaster. If the mule got excited and tried to get up, he could be in real trouble. I couldn't push him back because he might go nuts. I decided to back off and let the mule figure it out for himself. I tied the Appaloosa, unsaddled, then sat on a bale of straw and watched the mule from a distance. The damn thing lay motionless for better than half an hour.

The sun was good and up and the animal hadn't moved a muscle. The horses were getting antsy, waiting for breakfast.

Gus came from the house. "You're back. What are you doing?"

"I'm watching one of god's creations," I said.

Gus looked over at the mule. "What's he doing?"

"Hell if he knows." I stood and stretched. "I guess I'll feed everybody. I'll be inside in a while."

"You want flapjacks?"

"Sounds great," I said.

I made the rounds, throwing hay, scooping grain, dumping bad water, filling troughs with good water. When I came back to the mule's paddock, he was still in the same pathetic position. I dropped a couple flakes in the mule's feeder and left for the house.

The mule was planted in that spot until near noon, when, while no one was looking, he must have squirmed his way out. He'd walked to the house and stood there staring at the back door.

I'd been watching what piece of him I could see from the kitchen window off and on. "Gus, you're not going to believe this," I said.

Gus looked out the window. "I wouldn't ride that thing if you paid me in American dollars. He's spooky."

I went outside, walked to the animal, stood briefly in front of him, then walked on past him to the barn. The mule heeled like a dog.

FOUR

DUNCAN CAMP'S giant horse was slowly coming around. He tried to walk over me a couple times on the lead rope, but a well-placed pointy stick had put an end to that nonsense. I'd tied the horse's head high at the kickboard and irritated him with bags of cans, rustling plastic and even a gas-powered weed cutter. He showed wide-eyed panic at the introduction of anything new, but then began to settle down. He couldn't get away and he wasn't being eaten by anything. That morning, after fifteen minutes of stretching out my own muscles, trying to work out the tension of anticipation and ward off injury, I saddled Felony and climbed onto his back in the round pen. I could feel he was wired, but he rode like a dream, cantering clockwise and anti-clockwise equally well, pulling for quick, if not sliding, stops, backs. He even did a side pass on a moderately gentle cue. So, I opened the gate, took a deep breath, and rode out into the yard, then into the big field. The big horse felt good, a little too tense to be smooth, but he responded quickly. Before an elk could pop out from behind a bush or a helicopter appear out of nowhere, I took Felony back to the barn and let the short ride remain a good one. I brushed him out for a long time, talking to him, and he pushed at me with his nose. I could feel him relaxing. I didn't give him a treat, only scratched his belly. I don't think there's a better feeling in the world than having a big, scared animal relax around you. I untied him and walked him back to his stall.

As I walked out of the barn, I tossed a look at the mule. He was munching happily in his new indoor quarters.

That afternoon, after a few long hours in the pasture getting the rest of my hay, I saddled Felony for a longer ride. I left Zoe in the house with Gus. I didn't need her giving him a start by darting off after a rabbit or chipmunk. I rode west out onto the BLM land adjacent to my place, just east of the Red Desert. It was dramatic land, dry, remote, wild. It was why I loved the West. I had no affection necessarily for the history of the people and certainly none for the mythic West, the West that never existed. It was the land for me. And maybe what the land did to some who lived on it.

I rode along in the shadow of a butte, protecting myself from the intense afternoon sun. Ahead I saw something odd. On the red soil, the black was out of place, so I approached slowly for a closer look. Right over it, I still wasn't sure what I was seeing. But as I dismounted it came together for me. The ears and the shape of the face were easy to see once seen. The coyote had been burnt. I touched the charred remains and put my fingers to my nose. I thought I could smell gasoline. Whether I smelled it or not, I knew what had happened. Someone had poured fuel down into the animal's den and tossed in a match. It was something sheepherders did occasionally; they hated coyotes.

I looked around and found tire tracks about twenty yards away. They were the tracks of a dually pickup; that much was clear. The impression of the rear tires was nearly as deep as the front, so the bed must have been loaded. A heavy load, I guessed. I followed the tracks backward and located the coyote's lair on a steep place on the butte's face. The entrance was blackened from the fire. The coyote had run a hundred yards aflame and whoever had struck the match had followed along in the truck, watching. I felt sick. I was confused, near tears, angry. No one was keeping sheep there, so the lame excuse of protecting stock didn't even make sense.

Then I heard them. The whimpering seemed to come from nowhere at first and for a second I imagined it to be the last ghost sounds of the dead coyote. I listened and traced the whimpering to a clump of sage and there in the shade and red dust were two pups, smoke darkened, eyes just opened. They could not have been more than two weeks old. One, a female, had a badly burned foreleg, but she was moving with slightly more strength than her intact brother. I wet my kerchief with water from my canteen and tried to wring drips into the pups' mouths. Their little tongues weakly lapped at their lips. I put them in my saddlebags and mounted.

I loped along, checking on the babies every few minutes. I tried to keep them wet, cool. They were no longer whimpering, but they were still alive. I also poured water over my saddlebags to soak the leather. I tried to shake the image of the mother dog from my head. She had no doubt been between her pups and the den opening and had tried to carry the fire out and away with her.

When I cantered up to the back door, Gus came rushing out before I was off the horse. He knew something was wrong because I never rode an animal hard up to the barn.

"What's the trouble?" Gus asked.

"I found some coyote pups. They're injured." I opened the pouch with the babies and he looked in with me.

"What do you want me to do?" he asked.

I blew out a breath, collecting myself. I looked at Gus. I couldn't trust Felony alone with the old man. The horse might walk over him. "You take the pups into the kitchen. I'll take care of the horse."

Gus took the bags inside. I loosened Felony's girth and took off his bridle. I led him over to the hot walker and clipped him up, left to make slow circles while he cooled down. I grabbed my big first aid kit from the barn.

Back in the kitchen I could see that Gus had carefully unloaded the puppies onto the table. The little female with the burned leg actually managed to drag herself a couple inches. The male didn't move. I put my hand on the little body and felt no life. I stepped away from the table, poured myself a glass of water and drank it all down. I believed I was shaking, but I couldn't see it in the hand that held the glass.

Zoe was at the table, looking up with obvious concern.

Gus brought me back to where I needed to be. "Well, let's take care of this one," he said.

"Okay." I went back to the table. "Gus, go get me those little scissors you use for your mustache."

Gus left and was back quickly.

I clipped away the fur above the burned area. The left paw was pretty much gone. But there was no bleeding. I told myself that was a good thing. I couldn't believe the little girl was alive. I shook my head and looked over at Gus. "She ought to be dead," I said.

"She's tough." The way he said it I knew he was already forming an attachment to the animal.

Gus tried to call the small-animal vet in town without success. I'd hardly ever used him anyway. My horse vet, Oliver, was two hundred miles away doing some work for a pack outfit in the high country. I looked at the little coyote and imagined her as a tiny horse. I went to the refrigerator and got some antibiotics, divided what I would have given a horse by a thousand and injected it. Then I mixed up some sugar and warm water and asked Gus to try to get some of it into the pup. I thought it might help with the shock.

"You okay in here?" I asked.

Gus didn't look up. He used a dropper to put the sugar solution on the pup's lips. "I'm fine."

I called Zoe twice, but she wouldn't budge from Gus's side, so I left her. I went back out to put Felony away. With all my concern over the coyotes I hadn't given much thought to what Felony might unexpectedly do. The horse had been great, steady, and still felt so as I finished unsaddling him and led him to his stall.

I returned to the house and made a bed out of sheets in the corner of the study. Gus came in and put the pup down in the nest. Zoe came close and Gus stopped her. I put a hand on his shoulder. "Gus, let Zoe check her out."

Zoe sniffed the pup, then lay down, curling herself around the little thing. She gently licked at the burned leg.

"Maybe that's the best thing," Gus said.

I thought he was probably right.

Gus asked me if I was hungry and I told him I wasn't. He then made me a sandwich and I ate it. That night I slept in the den on the recliner. Zoe stayed put beside the coyote.

The next morning, the puppy was struggling to move a little more. She would take a step, become exhausted, and fall over. Zoe remained by her. Gus tried again with the sugar solution, then with some warm milk. The pup licked at her lips finally and I could see Gus's shoulders relax. I went out and fixed what needed fixing, worked a couple horses, then came back to check on the patient. I didn't want to go into town, but Gus pretty much pushed me out of the house.

No doubt because of the coyote, I was hating people more than usual as I drove into town. I drove past the Wal-Mart that I refused to enter, past the McDonald's that I refused to enter and past the church that I refused to enter. I glanced over at the parking lot of the Rusty Spur Motel, wondering if David Thayer's car was there. When I'd called to set up lunch with David, he sounded cool. But why not? I hadn't seen him since he was a kid. To him I was just some old fogey mate of his father's. That was true enough. I told him we'd meet at the Little Winds Café. I'd suggested it because it worked at some kind of cosmopolitan front and I thought David might appreciate the effort. But also the food was the best in Highland, though that statement in and of itself was not all that significant.

I arrived first. The hostess, an overly skinny cowgirl I remembered from the barrel-racing event at the summer rodeo, led me to a booth against the far wall.

"How's this, Mr. Hunt?" she asked.

"Just fine," I said. "You've got the drop on me though. I don't know your name."

"It's Becky."

"Thanks, Becky."

Highland was a small enough town that most people had a vague knowledge of who everyone was, but it did facilitate matters to be different in some way. In my case, in was the color of my skin. It could easily have been a problem for some folks, but it hadn't turned out to be. I, of course, realized that I was referred to as the "black rancher." I suppose had I been extremely handsome, I would have been the "good-looking, black rancher."

I studied the menu, remembering a time when I would not have needed the narrow specs perched on my nose that fit too tightly against my temples. From where I sat I could look across the room and out the window at the street and the storefronts on the other side. A monstrous SUV pulled up at Ken's Sporting Goods and four men got out, stretching and looking at the sky. I knew they were buying fishing licenses and I was a little envious. They were no doubt headed up into the Winds, with a stop first at the tribal office for permission, then the drive up. I considered the long drive through the reservation to the Owl Creek hills. The low, red and yellow ochre range always relaxed me, in spite of the heat, in spite of the arid desolation, probably because of it. I actually had a jar of soil from there on a shelf in my barn.

Two young men entered the restaurant. One was of medium height, about six feet, the other a littler taller and in the taller man I could see Howard's eyes and cheekbones. They wore jeans, new Western boots and short-sleeved shirts. They were not so differently dressed from others in town. They were healthy looking and strong enough, but their postures said they weren't ranch men. They walked like nothing really hurt.

I stood and signaled to them with a wave.

"John?"

"That's me." I shook David's hand. I could see his mother in his face.

David introduced me to his friend, Robert. Robert managed to seem aloof without looking away.

I nodded and shook the man's hand. "Come on, let's sit down," I said. I straightened the napkin in my lap and looked at David. "I can't believe you're all grown up. Last time I saw you, you were fifteen, I think. Considerably shorter."

David nodded.

"I don't mean to embarrass you," I said, "but what a long time. So, you're in college now?"

"University of Illinois," David said.

"Me, too," from Robert.

"How's your mother?" I asked.

"I suppose Dad told you."

"Yes, he did. I was sorry to hear about that. Is she okay?" I felt somehow caught, having attempted to play dumb.

David nodded, again.

"So, what brings you to the outskirts of no place?" I asked. I hated working at conversation, but he was my friend's kid and I wanted him to feel comfortable.

"We're here for a rally." David said.

"Rally? What kind of rally?"

The waitress came. She was obviously intrigued with the young men and she admired them while she named the specials. "The tortilla soup is real good," she said at the end of the list. "Well, I'll give you guys a few minutes."

David and Robert laughed a little.

"What is it?" I asked.

"Nothing," Robert said.

"What kind of rally?" I asked again.

"It's a gay pride rally," Robert said.

"I see." I took a sip of water.

"Because of the killing that took place here last week," David said.

I nodded. "Awful thing. When is this rally?"

"Tomorrow at noon." David ran a hand over his hair. "It's going to be in front of the city hall building. Tell me, what is this place like?"

"Place?" I asked.

"This town," Robert said.

I shrugged. "It's a little town. It's okay. Mostly white. Indians get treated like shit. You know, America. The murder hit everybody pretty hard."

Robert might have smirked. I felt it as much as I saw it.

"My father's a bastard," David said. It came out of nowhere and not.

I studied his eyes.

"He screwed around and hurt my mother. He had an affair. He didn't think about her or me or anything."

"I didn't know that," I said.

David was staring at me, as if somehow I was representing his father at that moment. "He's a real bastard," he said again.

Robert leaned in, perhaps to break the tension. "So, what do you do here?"

"I raise and train horses," I told him. "I've got a ranch about thirty miles from town. I used to run cattle, but not anymore."

"How do you know David's father?" Robert asked.

I glanced at David. "We were at college together. Berkeley."

"Berkeley?" Robert asked.

"You find that odd?"

"John studied art history," David said. "Right?"

I nodded, a bit surprised that David knew and remembered that fact.

"So, why are you here?" Robert asked.

I looked out the window, then to Robert. As my father would have said, there was a tone to his question. "Did you notice the landscape when you drove in?" I asked. "This is a beautiful place." I pulled back some. "I love horses. This is where I grew up. Well, down in Colorado." I shrugged. "Where are you from?"

"Vermont," Robert said.

"Pretty state," I said. "I went to school in New Hampshire."

"I thought you went to Berkeley."

"I went to prep school in New Hampshire. Phillips Exeter." I felt bad for enjoying the confusion and disappointed assumptions re-flected in Robert's face. "Sometimes they let us country boys out. Anyway, it's too green back there in New England for me."

"How big is your ranch?" David asked.

"I've sold half of it and the BLM leases since I don't run cattle anymore. So, there's about fifteen hundred acres. Not so big."

Robert asked, "How many black people live out here?"

I was a little startled by the question. "Good question. I don't know. How many black people live in Chicago?"

Robert stumbled.

"I've never counted people around here, Robert. Black or white. A whole bunch of Indians live over that way."

"Ever have any problems?" Robert asked. "With race, I mean."

"Of course I have, son. This is America. I've run into bigotry here. Of course, the only place anybody ever called me nigger to my face was in Cambridge, Mass." I let that sink in. "There are plenty of stu-pid, narrow-minded people around. They're not hard to find. There are a lot of ignorant people, a lot of good, smart people. Is it differ-ent where you come from?"

Robert laughed nervously, but avoided my question by drinking some water.

I felt a little like a bully and I didn't like it. I was a bit on the de-fensive and I liked that even less. I made myself relax, as when on a nervous horse. I viewed it as good practice.

"I'm here because I like the West," I said.

The waitress returned.

"I'll just have the burger," David said.

"Same for me," from Robert. He dropped his hand on top of David's on the table.

The waitress couldn't help but see this and it registered slightly on her young face. "Cheese on those?" she asked.

"No, thanks," David said.

Robert shook his head.

"Becky, I'll have the BLT without the B and with avocado," I said. "And I'll have cottage cheese instead of the fries."

"Be right up," Becky said.

"Don't tell me you're a vegetarian," Robert said.

"Okay," I said. "So, what do you think of our little town?"

"Not much to it," David said.

"That's for damn sure," I agreed. I looked out the window and saw that the SUV was gone from in front of the sporting goods store.

"So, why did you study art history?" Robert asked.

"I like art." I emptied my water glass and set it back down. "What are the two of you studying?"

"Undecided," Robert said, somewhat sheepishly.

"There's plenty of time," I told him.

"I'm majoring in English right now," David said. "So, how did you and my father get together? He was a business major."

"I don't remember. Probably some anti-war protest or something." I leaned back. I felt slightly sleepy. "You two should come out to my place. I'll put you on a couple horses and you can really see this country." I considered that I was forgetting why they were there and I felt a little stupid. "So, when is the rally again?"

"Tomorrow at noon," David said.

"You think folks would mind if some straight cowboys showed up?"

"I don't think so," David said.

The waitress brought the food and we began to eat.

I looked at the two young men together. They were handsome, bright. I thought about Howard.

"How does your father feel about your being gay?" I asked.

The directness of my question caused David to glance at Robert. "He doesn't like it."

"He hates it," Robert said.

"Sorry to hear that," I said.

"How do you feel about it?" David asked me.

"I don't feel one way or the other about it," I said. "Should I?"

"No," David admitted.

"I hope I didn't offend you," I said.

"You didn't." David fiddled with his napkin.

"Would you like to come to my place for dinner tomorrow? It's a bit of a ride. I'll drive you out and you can stay over if you like."

David questioned Robert with a look.

"Listen, no rush," I said. "You can let me know tomorrow."

"Okay," David said.

We finished lunch, which turned out to be a dragging, boring affair. Still, I liked Howard's son. I tried not to dislike Robert. I wasn't put off by the men's homosexuality, but Robert's display for the benefit of the waitress seemed mean-spirited. I didn't feel bad for thinking that, as I considered I would have been as put off by a heterosexual man or woman similarly marking territory.

I was in my Jeep, pulling off the highway and headed up the hill to Morgan's house.

Morgan's mother was on her knees in the garden in front of the house. She pushed herself to standing as I approached.

"Good day, Emily," I said. "New knee pads?"

"What I need is new knees."

"You wouldn't like the new ones," I told her. "What are you up to? Dividing irises?"

"Yes," she said with disgust. "I'm sorry I ever put them in. They're pretty but every time I turn around I'm dividing them again. How would you like to take a hundred home with you?"

"I don't think so. Not with that testimonial. Is that wild, good-for-nothing daughter of yours around?"

"Barn," Emily said.

I left Emily to her irises and walked around the house, across the corral to the barn. I found Morgan in the tack room, cleaning her bridle.

"I heard some people really do that," I said. "Me, I like to let my tack get all cracked and brittle."

She put down the sponge and stepped close, stood there, arms at her sides. "So, what are the ground rules? Do we kiss when we greet now?"

"I reckon. Till you get tired of me." I put my hands on her shoulders and kissed her lips. Her mouth was soft, sweet. I liked kissing her.

Morgan turned away and went to hang her bridle on the wall. Again facing me, she said, "I guess we're going to have to have sex soon."

"Sounds reasonable," I said. "It's been on my mind."

"Well, I'm glad to hear that, Hunt. I've been trying to figure just how retarded in these matters you are."

I looked around at the neat room, the clean saddles and tack arranged in a way that made sense. "You sure you want to get tied up with a slob like me?"

"No."

I laughed. "Your mother looks good."

"The man-stealer," she hissed.

"Hey, guess what I've got at my house? I've found a baby coyote."

"Where'd you find him?"

"Over in the desert. Some asshole torched a den and killed the mother. I found two, but one died. I hope this little girl makes it. She has a burned leg."

"I hate people," Morgan said.

"They're no damn good, that's for certain. I was so pissed off."

Morgan was silent.

"Anyway, I came over—"

She cut me off, "For sex?"

"Well, no." She'd caught me off guard, which apparently was not difficult to do. "I came over to ask you out on a date, sort of." I sat on a stool.

"Sort of?" she said. "Already I don't know how I can resist."

"Give me a break, sweetie." The "sweetie" just came out. It felt easy saying it and I could see it soften Morgan. "There's a memorial service for the kid who was murdered. "I just had lunch with an old friend's kid and his boyfriend, partner I guess, and I'm going to go to this thing. Rally."

"How was lunch?"

"It was fine," I said. "At one point I felt a little defensive and I feel bad about that."

"People are usually defensive when there's something to be defensive about," Morgan said.

I nodded.

"His being gay bother you?" she asked.

"You know, that's the thing. I don't think it did, but I'm not sure. I don't care at all about that stuff, but I have to admit I wasn't completely comfortable."

"Yeah, but you're uncomfortable around me most of the time," she said.

"Point taken," I said. "Anyway, they were okay. I'm just an old fart who doesn't get out much." I slid off the stool. "I'd better get moving. I've got a few horses to work yet." I stepped to the door. "So, tomorrow?"

"Sure."

"Dinner, tomorrow night as well. Emily's invited, too."

"She'll like that," Morgan said.

We walked back to the front of the house. Emily was talking to the white-haired kid who delivered her groceries while he leaned over the exposed engine of his little truck.

"What's up, Cotton?" Morgan asked.

"Oh, I'm looking for this damn leak," he said. "I gotta put antifreeze in this thing every time I turn around."

"I told him to check his water pump," Emily said.

Cotton ran a hand through his hair and left a streak of grease. "It's got to be leaking, but I can't find it. I put newspaper under it every night and nothing, not a single drip."

I looked in the back of the truck and saw the gallon jugs of antifreeze. "Hey, Cotton, you ever see white smoke come out your exhaust?"

Cotton looked up from his engine and at me. "Yeah."

Morgan, Emily and I said, together, "Blown head gasket."

With that, Emily turned back to her gardening.

"Pick you up at eleven," I said to Morgan.

I arrived home to get the latest coyote puppy update from Gus. He was sitting on the floor by the pup and Zoe. I knelt beside him.

"She's taking more of the warm milk and she's a lot stronger. She's moving more but not much. She tires pretty quickly then drifts back to sleep. Still sounds like her breathing is labored. Smoke."

"Thanks, doc."

"She's a cute little thing." Gus was in love with her.

"She is that," I said.

"I wish I could get my hands on those bastards," Gus said.

I nodded. "I guess I'd better build a kennel crate of some kind next week. In case she makes it."

"She's a fighter," Gus said. "She's going to make it. And Zoe won't get ten feet from her."

"I wonder how this is going to work," I said. "After all, this is a wild animal, Gus."

"Right now she's just a pound of misery," he said.

"Okay, Gus, I read you." I stood. "Well, I'm going to work. You're in charge."

"Hell, I'm always in charge. Sometimes I'm the only one who knows it, but I'm always in charge."

I was on Felony and things were going pretty well. I felt good about the animal after the last long and desperate ride. The big horse was at ease in the open field, loping along, then coming to a jog trot.

It began with a twitch just behind the girth. I sensed it more than I felt it and I thought to turn the horse, to distract him and disengage his hind end, but my thought was slow finishing. Felony planted for a second then took off toward the fence of the big pasture. I seesawed the reins with increasing pressure, pulled on one rein and then the other, but I couldn't pull him up or slow him down. I had another hundred yards before the fence and so I let the horse run, gave him his head and even urged him on. I just went with it. About thirty yards from the fence, and a real back wreck, I gently squaw-reined Felony left and the animal went with me, even slowing some. I kicked him a little and the horse opened up again. I let him run the length of the open area. I didn't let him burn his tank though, but he was good and ready to stop when I asked him to whoa. I walked him some, let him lope, then took him back to the same spot where he had spooked. I had no idea what had gotten into him, but I'd made a breakthrough.

As I rode the horse in a walk back to the barn, I considered the fact that I didn't have many wrecks left in my old body. I felt a wave of fear and then I felt the horse respond, felt the big muscles tense. I let my body melt and immediately the horse relaxed. I tightened my muscles on purpose and got no reaction. I tried to think back to what I was thinking just before Felony had blown up. I'd had an unpleasant memory, maybe of my wife's death, I didn't really know, but I'd had something bad go through my mind. I couldn't believe that the horse had sensed it. I thought about Susie's death again. Nothing. I thought about calling Wallace Castlebury's brother. Nothing. I thought about having sex with Morgan. Felony tightened. All I could do was shake my head. I had to train this horse to tolerate the troubling thoughts of his rider. This was too much.

I took Felony back out into the field and thought through as many scary things as I could find. I thought about Gus getting sick, about getting thrown, about sex, about lunch with David and Robert, about bad snowstorms. I was confusing the hell out of the poor horse, but that was what I wanted. I'd clear my mind and he'd relax. I'd have to do this everyday for a while. My fear was, however, that all these things would cease to bother me. I gave Felony a rub on the neck, got off, loosened his girth, and walked him back to the barn.

FIVE

WEATHER WALLY on the radio called for periods of heavy rain, but it was the stiffness in Gus's knees that had me believing it was coming. The breeze was bracing out of the northwest and I remembered seeing snow this early. I spent the morning getting the barns and paddocks ready for wet weather, digging trenches along the perimeters of shelters, filling in low spots, pretty much trying to forestall anything that nature was going to do anyway. The mule had gotten out again and spent the wee hours munching at the alfalfa bales. I put him in a stall in the barn and gave him a half feeding.

Back in the house, I found Gus sitting at the kitchen table, sewing a ripped shirt pocket. I absently studied the project over the old man's shoulder. "You sew like I weld," I said.

"Yeah, but I'm old."

"Are you sure you don't want to ride into town?" I asked. "I don't plan to be there very long."

"I'm sure. I'm gonna stay here and crank up the heat. Maybe that will make my knees feel better."

"Sounds good," I said. "Well, I'd better make myself presentable if I'm going to pick up a young lady."

"Good luck," Gus said. "With the getting-presentable part."

The sky teased as I drove to Morgan's. Emily was standing in her garden, surveying. She wore an apron that read *Born to Be Old.*

"Morning, Emily."

Emily nodded.

"What are you doing?" I asked.

"Saying good-bye to everybody, my flowers," she said. She looked at the sky. "Because as sure as dogs are smarter than people, it's gonna snow."

"Why do you think that?"

"It ain't because of Weather Wally, I can tell you that. That idiot is calling for rain. That sky is full of snow." She pointed up. "The hawks tell me. They've been circling all morning."

Morgan came from the house and down the porch steps. "Don't listen to her," Morgan said. "Those hawks are always up there."

"Yes and no," Emily said. "So, where are you two off to?"

"We're going to a rally in town," I told her.

"What rally?"

"A gay and lesbian rally."

Emily frowned. "What will they think up next? Well, have fun. Of course, that's my general advice about everything." She turned back to her garden. "Good-bye, gaillardia."

In town, I parked my rig on a street off the main drag and we walked a short block to the square. Only a few people had begun to assemble. There were some blankets laid out on the lawn where box lunches waited. A couple of deputies stood near the entrance to the Town Hall, but they didn't give the appearance of guarding the place. Deputy Hanks was strolling the sidewalk. The air had turned cold and most were wearing jackets. A podium was set on the landing halfway up the Hall steps. A television news crew from Casper was lazily putting together equipment, laying out cables and setting up tripods. Morgan and I were the first to sit on the thirty or so chairs that had been set up in uneven rows at the bottom of the steps.

"We're early," I said.

"We're not that early," Morgan said.

I shrugged. "This is really sad, isn't it? For someone to get killed like that. To kill somebody any way is sad."

Morgan looked around. "There are just few enough people to make this creepy. Maybe it's the weather."

"Maybe," I said.

David and Robert came into view, turning onto the block.

I pointed with my eyes. "There's David."

Morgan turned to see. "Good-looking boys."

The men were huddled together, in only light sweaters against the cold. They had come in September expecting the summer warmth to persist the way it might in other places.

"They must be freezing," Morgan said.

"I suspect so."

"Which one is David?"

"On the right."

"Handsome," she said.

"Well, he's attached," I said. "What am I? Chopped liver?"

"More or less."

"I don't know which is more insulting," I said. "More or less."

I stood and tried to catch David's attention, but my wave went unnoticed. A couple of men rapidly approached David and Robert from the other side of the street. One was rangy with a shock of dark hair and the other was tall but stout. They wore jeans, boots, T-shirts, and no jackets. I observed David's body stiffen and in the young man's face, for the first time, I could really see Howard.

"What's going on?" Morgan asked.

"I don't know." I had already started to move off in their direction, trying to run without running.

"John?" Morgan was frightened.

I could see but not hear the exchange of words. The rangy redneck pushed Robert, of a sudden, two open hands to the chest. Robert fell back a step or two and regained his balance.

The deputy, Hanks, was there before me, inserting his wide body into the middle of the trouble. By the time I got there, Hanks was shooing the rednecks away, roughly. He had his hands in the middle of their backs and had pushed them halfway across the street.

The man who had pushed Robert shouted out, "Faggot!" and Hanks gave him an extra shove that sent him to his knees. He got up, then loaded with his friend into a rusting, mid-seventies BMW.

I asked Robert if he was all right.

Hanks came loping back. "Sorry about that," he said. It was a sincere apology, though it wasn't clear whether he was apologizing for the actions of the thugs or for our village.

"Yeah, right," Robert said sarcastically. His face was still red.

Hanks pulled away from us, then walked again toward the BMW. The wiry man put the car in gear and peeled away.

"Pigs," Morgan said.

David put a hand on Robert's shoulder, but he jerked back, twisting his body at the waist. Then he paced off, looked up at the sky and just screamed. Everyone up and down the street and in front of the Town Hall turned to the noise. Deputy Hanks's back had been turned and the scream gave him a start. He pivoted to run back, but stopped. I waved the deputy off, letting him know that everything was under control.

David approached Robert again, stepped behind him, and put a hand on his back. Robert didn't pull away this time.

"What kind of fucking place is this?" Robert asked. He shot a look at me. "Tell me."

I felt embarrassed.

Just then, snow began to fall.

I looked at the sky, flat and gray, and a flake landed on my face and melted. When I looked back at Robert I saw that his eyes were moist. I turned away, afraid to make him self-conscious by noticing. The townspeople, what few had come, began to leave their seats. Others who had laid out blankets, folded up and started to depart as well. They had all been willing to brave the cold, but the snow was too much. The news crew was quickly disassembling their equipment while the reporter sat in the passenger side of the satellite truck having an animated conversation on his cellular phone.

"This doesn't look good," Morgan said.

I wasn't sure whether she was referring to the storm or the sudden and premature end to the rally. Whatever, I responded, "No, it doesn't." To David and Robert. "We've got to get you two something warmer to wear."

"We didn't expect the weather to turn," David said.

"I've got extra jackets at my house," I said. "Why don't we just ride on out there now?"

David turned to Robert, his body language asking for his feeling.

"I don't care," Robert said. "You decide."

"Okay," David said to me.

Unfortunately, I'd forgotten how cold it was in the back of my Jeep. Morgan and I were roasting in the front while David and Robert huddled beneath the blanket I kept stowed under the seat. The snow had fallen heavily for about twenty minutes and was now tapering off. It was just beginning to stick on the light green leaves of the sage that grew along the highway.

"So, what do you guys call this?" David asked.

"September," Morgan said.

"Warming up at all back there?" I fiddled with the heat controls, not that I could push the lever any farther to the right.

"Not really," David said.

I looked at the weather and then at Morgan. "I'll drop you off. What do you think?"

"You probably should. I'll try to keep Mother from running out naked in the snow."

"Need anything done with your animals?" I asked.

"No, I've got it covered. Anyway, there's still plenty of light left."

I looked at the boys in the mirror. "You guys mind if dinner becomes lunch and I drive you back before it's too late?"

"Makes sense," David said.

I dropped off Morgan and let the two men stay in the back under the blanket. Soon, we were rolling down the trail to my place.

"It's beautiful," David said.

"It's work is what it is," I said. I looked at it. It was especially beautiful under the dusting of snow.

I halted the Jeep in front of the house and watched the mule come walking out of the barn toward me. "Have mercy," I said, shaking my head.

"What is it?" David asked.

"The devil himself," I said.

"What?"

"Nothing. Come on, let's get you two warmed up. Gus said he'd have the heat cranked up today." Gus must have forced Zoe out of the house for her daily business because she came trotting over to me. She sat at my feet and awaited her command. "This is Zoe," I said. "Greet, Zoe."

Zoe went to the strangers and got a noseful.

David patted her head. "She's well trained."

"She's smart," I said. "She makes me look good."

Gus met us at the door. "Can you believe it," the old man said. "Snow! I tell you weather has no respect."

"Gus, David and Robert."

"Howdy." Gus shook Robert's hand and then David's. "Your hands are like ice. Where are your coats?"

"Don't have any," David said.

"Get your asses in there by the fire," he barked. "No coats. What the Sam Hill is that all about?"

"We're doing lunch instead of dinner," I said. "That all right?"

"That's fine. No coats."

"How's our patient?"

"She's dragging herself around pretty good, now. I had to push Zoe outside. I've been giving the little girl warm milk from a rubber glove. I pierced a finger and she really goes after it."

"That's great, Gus." I made a move toward the door.

"Where the hell are you going?"

"I'm going out there and I'm going to tie that mule's legs together. How the hell did he get out?"

"He was out as soon as you left. I caught him and stuck him in a paddock, but there he is. He's a spooky one."

"Well, I'm sticking that son of a bitch back in a stall and I'm going to weld the damn gate shut. If he gets out again, then he's just going to have roam around loose. I can't be worrying about him all the goddamn time."

Gus had started away in the middle of my rant and was asking David and Robert if they wanted coffee.

"Yeah, go ahead and walk away from me while I'm talking," I said. I liked that Gus didn't have time for anyone's carryings on.

I was pleased to find myself outdoors and alone. The snowflakes were swirling, the cold front getting confused by the wall of heat offered by the Red Desert. I took this as a sign that the storm wouldn't amount to much. Unfortunately, my taking it as a sign meant that we were in for a dumping, my guesses about weather were almost always misguided. The mule was waiting for me about halfway to the barn and he heeled to me like a dog and ambled agreeably into a stall when I swung open the door. "Okay, you candidate for the glue factory," I said. I had to be impressed by the animal. I secured the gate with a nose chain, then tied a rag in a hard knot around the chain's clasp. "You get out of that and you can sleep in the house." I realized my light jacket was becoming inadequate for the weather, another indication that my perceived sign had been characteristically wrong. I walked quickly through the barn and checked everybody's water before heading back inside.

Gus had pulled a load of coats from the closet and put them in a pile on the floor. He and the guests were picking through them.

"What's going on here?" I asked.

"Trying to find these boys some proper outerwear," Gus said. "Something toasty for the remainder of summer."

"Outerwear?"

"That's what they call it in the stores and the catalogs. You ought to know that—jacket man."

David laughed.

That fed Gus. "This man loves jackets. He's a pathetic addict. He can't pass one up."

"That's not true," I said.

Gus gestured to the pile on the floor. "None of these are mine." The old man paused for effect. "I rest my case."

"It gets cold around here," I said.

"Take your pick," Gus said to David and Robert. "The man's got no favorites. One's the same as the next."

The younger men looked to me. I waved them on. "Have at it," I said. "He's right. I need help, a twelve-sleeve program or something. Find something warm, though. You're going to need it."

"Bad out there?" Gus asked.

"Could be," I said.

"Hey, I wanted to ask you about the painting on the wall," Robert said.

"What about it?"

"Is it a Klee?"

"It is."

"A real Klee?"

"Yep. A real little Klee." I walked over to the small canvas. "And on that other wall is a Kandinsky watercolor. But that's the extent of my art collection."

"How much is the Klee worth?" Robert asked.

I bristled, but not noticeably. "I never think about it. I'm sure its value goes up and down. Why? You want to buy it?"

"No, I was just wondering." Robert laughed nervously. He turned back to the pile of jackets.

Gus watched the men try on the coats. "Did you know the boy who was killed?" he asked.

Robert shook his head.

"Terrible thing," Gus said.

"We had some truck with the boy they arrested," Gus said.

David stood. He was swallowed by a yellow slicker. He looked at Gus and then at me.

"I think I'm a little wider than you, son," I said. "Besides, that will keep you dry, but not warm."

"You met the guy?" David asked, peeling off the garment.

"He actually did a little work for me around here," I said, embarrassed by the association.

"Little is the operative word," Gus said. "Showed up out of nowhere. He wasn't so much weird as he was slow."

"He was dumber than a bucket of hair," I said. "Still, I can't imagine his doing such a thing. Hell, I can't imagine anybody doing it."

"We put up with people like that all the time." Robert's tone was only slightly strident.

"I'm sorry," I said.

Then it was as if Robert realized for the first time or again that Gus and I were black. He fell back into himself.

"Don't worry about it, Robert," I said. "Nobody's got the hate market cornered in this country."

"Yeah," said Gus. "There's plenty of hate for everybody. Rally round the flag, boys."

Robert smiled weakly, then turned his attention to a down-filled parka with purple pockets.

"Now that will keep you warm," I said.

"It had better," Gus sneered. "As ugly as that thing is."

I walked to the window and peered out. Just as I had predicted, counter to my prediction the wind was really blowing and the snow was really falling. "It's an official mess out there," I said. "I hope you boys don't mind staying the night. I'd rather not risk your lives and mine on that road in this storm in the dark."

Robert gave David an uneasy look, but David didn't notice or simply didn't respond.

David said, "That's fine." When David did look at Robert, Robert looked away. "Robert?"

"Sounds okay. Thanks, John."

"You bet."

While Gus prepared the meal, I took David and Robert, in their new coats, out to see the barns and horses. We wandered through the long barn and out the other end. The friendly horses shoved their heads out into the alley, looking for treats or just a rub on the nose.

"How many do you have?" David asked.

"Twenty-five," I said. "A nice even odd number. But they're not all mine. Several I'm training for other people. When winter comes, I'll take the shoes off most of my guys and turn them out."

"When winter comes?" Robert laughed.

"Son, this ain't winter," I said in my cowboy voice. "This here is sun-bathing weather."

"This must be a lot of work," David said. We were in the small barn now. The wind was spinning the vents above us.

"Nobody ever drowned in his own sweat," I said. I led them to the end of the middle barn. "And this is Felony." The horse pushed out his head. I was a little surprised by it. I stroked his nose. "He belongs to a neighbor."

"Felon?" David asked.

"Felony," I said. "Which of course is a much nicer name than Felon. The man's daughter named him. He's been a bit of a problem for them. He's a looker though. And he's coming along."

"That's what you do, train horses?" Robert asked.

There was a coolness between Robert and me that I didn't like. But also, I didn't much care, so I let it stand. "Now and again," I said.

"What's Felony's problem?" David asked. He reached out and rubbed the horse's nose.

"Basically, he's a nut. It's not so much that he thinks he's a person as he doesn't know that people aren't horses. That's a bad thing. Like I said, he's making progress. Or I'm making progress, I should say."

"You and Gus take care of this whole place?" David asked.

"Mostly. I hire a hand from time to time. They come and go. How'd you like a job?"

Robert laughed.

"I'm afraid you wouldn't want me," David said. "I don't know how to do anything."

"You can learn," I said. "Are you boys cold?"

"I'm fine," David said.

"Well, I'm cold," I said. "Let's get inside and grab some grub. How's that for authentic regional yak?"

In the kitchen, Gus had the table set. I could smell the chili. Zoe was in the corner lying on her bed, curled around the coyote pup. The pup pushed and whined, trying to get purchase on one of Zoe's dry teats.

"I see you moved our little patient," I said, stomping my boots clean in the mud room.

"More light in here," Gus said. He looked out the window over the sink. "The snow's not going to be all that bad. It's tapering off a little already."

"All I know is it's cold out there," I said.

Gus turned to David and Robert who were sitting at the table. "The coldest I've ever been was thirty-three in Phoenix. Not even a freeze and I thought I might cry, I was so cold." He pulled a ladle from the drawer and dropped it in the pot. "Come and sit down, ugly." This was to me.

"That coyote is really cute," David said as I sat.

"She's something, all right."

"How did you find her?" David watched Zoe with the pup.

"Some idiot torched her den and killed her mother," I said. "Her little brother didn't make it."

"Beautiful people," Robert said.

I nodded.

Robert put his hand on top of David's on the table.

"I didn't make the chili super hot," Gus said. "I didn't want to hurt anyone. There's Tabasco if anyone needs it."

"It smells great," David said.

"Gus can actually cook," I said.

"What do you mean by that?" Gus said.

"Well, to look at you, one wouldn't, well, never mind."

"You're lucky you're getting to eat at all," the old man said. Gus didn't take chili, but filled his bowl with salad.

"Aren't you having any chili?" David asked.

"Stuff gives me heartburn," Gus said.

"Since when?" I asked.

"Everybody eat up," he said. "I'm happy with leaves and bread. The bread's not great. I'm still working on that."

We ate for a while in silence. I tore off a piece of the crusty bread and studied the sleeping puppy. "You know, Gus, I think you're right. That little girl is going to pull through."

"Tough," Gus said.

"Did you want to call either of your parents?" I asked David.

"Certainly not my father," he said. "My mother's away on business."

"These things happen," Gus said. "People live, people die, people split up, people stay together and make each other miserable. Me, I've got ugly and he gets to live with me."

Robert laughed.

"Your mother's a special person," I said to David.

"Not special enough, I guess," David said. He poked at his chili with his spoon. "Why does my father hate me? He hates homosexuals. I'm a homosexual. It follows that he hates me. That's logic, right?"

I didn't say anything.

"I think the leg is going to fall off," Gus said.

"What are you talking about?" I asked.

"The coyote. I was looking at it and I think it has to fall off. Do you think we should cut it off?"

"Maybe, but not in the middle of a meal," I said.

"I didn't mean right now."

"All right, let's take a look at it later tonight. We might have to perform a little surgery."

We ate for a while.

"So, your being a homosexual's not a problem for your mother?" Gus asked, slapping butter on his bread. Gus had a way of cutting right to the chase.

"She's cool with it," David said.

"She says," Robert added.

"I believe she is." David put down his fork. "She's got her own stuff right now. Do you know why they broke up?"

I shook my head. "All of this is brand new to me."

"Well, I don't know either. I don't think my mother knows. That's what's so hard about all of this."

"Sounds hard," I said. I put down my fork and wiped my mouth. "Well, now that I've eaten, I think I'll go out and shovel the shit of large animals." I snapped my fingers for Zoe to come.

"I hope that's not a crack," Gus said.

David laughed.

"You guys want to join me in the freezing cold or stay in here where it's nice and toasty and have hot chocolate? You're not obliged to help."

"I'll help," David said.

"I think I'll sit in the other room with the fire," Robert said. "I have a bit of a headache."

"You want some aspirin or ibuprofen?" Gus asked.

"No, thanks."

Outside, Zoe led the way to the barn. The snow had all but stopped falling. That silence that snow brings had fallen.

"What kind of dog is Zoe?" David asked.

"She's a heeler. Some people call them Australian cattle dogs." I whistled and Zoe looked back. "Zoe, go find a rope, girl." Zoe trotted off into the barn, then came back with a lead rope in her mouth. "Good girl." I took the rope and gave her head a rub.

"That's pretty good," David said.

"I'd like to say I'm a great trainer, but Zoe's a genius."

I piled a deep cart with flakes of hay and asked David to push it down the aisle and put two flakes in each metal feeder. I checked the mule's gate and caught up to the cart. Once we had the hay tossed I started mucking out.

"I can help with that," David said.

"That's great. Grab a silage fork from over there and a bucket. Do the bay's stall."

"I thought you were married," David said.

"I was. My wife died."

"I'm sorry. I guess I knew that."

I waved him off. "You were a kid. Anyway, Gus came to live with me about six years ago. He's a big help."

"Gus is cool," David said.

"He is that." I rubbed at a stiffness in my neck. "Hey, I didn't mean to bring up any bad feelings earlier. You know, about your parents and all."

"The bad feelings aren't too far below the surface, I'm afraid." David paused to look in at Felony, the big palomino. "That's a big horse."

"An enormous baby," I said. "David, I don't know your mother very well at all. But I do know, or at least I used to know your father. He can be pretty rigid in his thinking."

"You got that right."

"I'm not just saying this to get on your good side, but sometimes it helps to hear that somebody else sees the same things you're seeing. Your father is a good person, but on occasion he can be a selfish—" I looked for a word.

"Jerk," David said.

"Not a word I would have used," I said. I looked up and down the aisle, as if afraid Howard might appear. "I lived with him. He's my friend, but he's sometimes clumsy when it comes to other people's feelings."

"And he's not tolerant of other people's ways," David said.

I nodded.

David looked at my eyes for a second, then we both laughed. "Well, you did get on my good side," he said.

"That wasn't my aim."

"So, why are you so tolerant?" he asked.

I shrugged. "I like to think I am. I'd like to think that if you were my son I'd behave differently from your father. But I can't honestly say that. You're not my son. I don't have a son."

"That's pretty honest," he said.

"Hey, I'm trying," I said.

"You know, my dad used to talk about you all the time like you were a god or something."

"I'm sorry to hear that," I said.

"Why?" he asked.

"I don't have much respect for gods."

"He used to say you could do anything, fix anything."

I looked at Felony, reached out and scratched his big nose. "Well, that's real flattering. It's not true, but it's flattering. Hey, it's getting cold out here. We'd better finish up and get back in that house before those two suck up all the heat."

Back in the house, Gus told us that Robert had decided to turn in for the night. David said he'd better go check on him.

Gus had scooped up the coyote puppy and had it lying on a nest of towels on the kitchen table. "That David's a nice man," he said.

"He is," I agreed.

"Robert's having a tough time." That was like Gus. He was generous of spirit. He wouldn't settle on thinking Robert was a jerk or an asshole, Gus just thought that this was difficult for him.

"Seems so," I said. I leaned over and examined the puppy. "So, you think we should just take that leg off."

"I think so. What do you think?"

"Well, it won't heal and become a leg she can use, that's for sure."

The tissue was thin and dark and the remaining piece looked as if it might fall off.

"Want me to go get your kit?"

"No, that's okay." I got a sharp knife from the drawer and went to the stove where I held the blade over a flame. I came back and sliced through the tissue. It was the smallest cut, but the largest as well. There would be no putting the leg back on. That was it. The slightest slash and now this animal had three legs instead of four.

"That's it?" Gus asked.

I looked for bleeding. There was none. "That's it."

"I could have done that," the old man said.

"We can all do a lot things," I said, "but we won't."

"I don't I think she felt it."

"I doubt she did," I said. "But who knows. Not that it matters now anyway. Let's try to get her through this alive." As I stood there watching Gus stroke the little head on the three-legged body, I realized that if the animal lived, she was a fixture. I couldn't very well put her into the wild. But she was wild. I'd have to find a way to socialize her and even then I knew I'd have to kennel her when new people came around. I got way ahead of myself in my thinking and tried to shake my head clear.

"What is it?" Gus asked.

"Nothing. You know, I think the little girl is going to make it."

"What's going on?" from David in the doorway.

"We just made a tripod," Gus said. "We cut off her leg. Well, John did, but hell I could have done it."

"Really?" David came over for a better look. "What will you do with the leg?"

Gus looked at me.

I'd intended to toss it into the garbage can beneath the sink, but now that suddenly seemed unceremonious. "I don't know," I said. "What does one do with a dead leg? I mean, it's not an animal."

"You weren't just going to toss it in the trash, were you?" Gus asked.

"What, do you want me to mount it on a plaque?" I looked at David and Gus looking at me. "I suppose I could bury it."

"That sounds right," Gus said.

"To me, too," David said.

"I suppose you expect me to say a few words over it as well. I mean, we're not having a funeral for a leg."

"No, of course not," Gus said.

"Give me that damn thing." I picked up the leg between my fingers and walked out of the kitchen. I was going to dig a little hole and drop it in.

And that's what I did, but before I tossed any dirt in on top of it, I said, "Well, little leg, I hope you're the last death the little girl has to see for a while." So, the leg had its funeral anyway.

The following morning was still and clear and not as cold as I thought it would be. The sun was rising in a cloudless eastern sky, but there were already clouds bunching up in the northwest. The snow stayed where it had drifted the night before. There was finally not much of it, just enough to quiet things, to muffle morning's naying for hay and grain. I was done feeding by the time David made his way down to the kitchen. Gus was preparing an uncharacteristically unhealthy breakfast of sausages and eggs.

"I have to say that smells great," I said. I looked over Gus's shoulder at the frying sausage. "When did you buy that?"

"It's not exactly meat," he said.

"What exactly is it?"

"Soy."

"Soy," I repeated.

"Soy sausage."

"Oh, lord." I shook my head. "You know, we've got some antelope steaks in the freezer."

"This is better for you."

"I'll try it."

"I'll bet those boys won't be able to tell the difference."

I walked over to Zoe and the puppy. "How's our patient this morning?" I asked.

"A little better, I think," Gus said. "She's really trying to drag herself around. I think somebody's coming down."

"Good morning," David said.

"David," I said.

Gus said, "Orange juice is in the fridge. Coffee's on the stove. We don't stand on ceremony around here."

"In other words," I said, "Get it your damn self."

David laughed and went for the fridge and the orange juice. "Breakfast smells terrific," he said as he pulled down a glass from the cupboard.

"Where's your . . ." Gus stopped, "what do you say? Partner? Boyfriend?"

"Boyfriend's good enough."

"Well, where the hell is he?" Gus asked.

"I don't think he slept too well." David sat at the table with his juice. "He's not usually in such a mood. I'm sorry"

I waved off David's apology. "Robert's okay."

I watched as David looked away out the window. He turned his attention to the puppy, but didn't say anything. There was sadness there and I didn't know what to say.

Gus set a plate in front of the boy and said, "Have at it while it's hot. Your boyfriend might have to fix his own breakfast if he's not down here pretty soon." He looked at me. "Put your butt in a chair."

I sat and looked at my plate. David had already started to eat. "How is it?" I asked.

"Good. I don't know what it is, but I like it."

"Don't know what what is?" Gus asked.

"This fake meat," David said.

"It's soy," I said.

"I like it," David said.

As we finished, a truck pulled up to the house. I stood and looked out. "That's Duncan," I said. "If you two gentlemen will excuse me."

I put on my jacket and walked outside.

"The snow is a good sign," Duncan said as a greeting. His daughter Ellie was with him. The young woman had spent a couple years down in Laramie at the university, but was taking a year off, she said.

"Good morning, Ellie," I said.

"Hi, Mr. Hunt."

"You make me feel old calling me that," I told her. We were all walking toward the barn.

"Sorry, Mr. Hunt."

"So, why is the snow a good sign?" I asked Duncan.

"I don't know. It's just a thing to say." Duncan put a cigarette in his mouth, but didn't light it. He often did that. "Daniel White Buffalo told me to tell you to give him a call."

"When did you see him?"

"I had to go out there. He claims that old Monday woman is stealing his cows. He claims that a lot. I suppose it's true, but I can't see it." Duncan was one of the few cattle detectives left in the area. White Buffalo is so bad at keeping records."

"And Clara Monday is smart," I said.

"Tougher than a dairy cow steak," Duncan said. "Rides around up there on that App with a thirty-thirty across her lap. She's gotta be seventy."

Ellie was stroking Felony's nose. The horse seemed grateful for the attention.

David came into the barn and joined us.

"Duncan, Ellie, this here is my friend David. He's from Chicago."

Duncan shook David's hand. "Where is Chicago?"

David looked to me.

"Just kidding you, son," Duncan said.

"How's he doing?" Ellie asked about Felony.

"He's going very well. You could ride him right now, but I don't know what he thinks of snow yet."

"He's a beautiful horse," David said.

"Thanks," Ellie said.

"Know much about horses?" Duncan asked.

"Nothing."

"If you're smart enough to say that, you're all right with me." Duncan put the cigarette he'd been fiddling with back into his pocket.

Robert came into the barn and we all looked his way. He walked up to David and gave him a kiss. I glanced at Duncan, looking for a reaction, then felt bad that I was doing that.

"Ellie, Duncan, this is Robert."

Robert nodded, but didn't offer his hand.

Ellie said, "Hello."

Duncan said, "Robert."

"The snow is beautiful, isn't it?" Robert said.

"Well, John," Duncan said, "Ellie just wanted to see her baby here. I guess we'll be going."

Robert decided to take offense. "Do we make you uncomfortable?"

David was as surprised as me at how confrontational Robert was being, especially with someone he didn't know. He was, however, less amused than I was. I looked to Duncan for his response.

"No, son," the big man said. "The two of you don't make me uncomfortable, but you alone do." Duncan was completely relaxed. "I'll give it to you in good old cowboy talk. I ain't never been around any homosexuals. Not to my knowledge, anyway. I'm just assuming that's what you are. I ain't never given it much thought, and I reckon I don't approve of it, but I can't say why. Still this is a free country and, to my mind, you can do what you want."

"Let's go, Daddy," Ellie said.

"Wait a second, darlin'," he said. "The man asked me a question."

"Son, I don't like anything thrown up in my face." He looked at David. "David, it was a pleasure meeting you."

Robert was angry. "Nice speech," he said.

Duncan smiled. "I don't lie. There are people around here who might shoot you for what you are. I don't know why, but I've no doubt that they would. People are bad like that and we've got our share. Maybe we've got more than our share, I don't know. Like I said, I believe this here is a free country. Now, my speech is over. See you later, John."

"Bye, Mr. Hunt," Ellie said.

I watched Duncan and his daughter leave the barn. What I liked about Duncan was that he was never out of control. He was a strange man in that he admitted to a lot of prejudices, but he never held that against himself.

David looked at Robert. I couldn't tell what was in him. He was confused, I knew that much, but whether he was angry with Duncan or with Robert, I simply had no clue. He shuffled his feet and walked over to scratch Felony's nose.

I probably should have said nothing, that would have been best, I knew it even then, but my mouth opened, "You just make friends everywhere you go." With that, I walked away. I didn't like feeling bad and this kid made me feel bad every time I turned around. This time I was feeling bad because I considered that I was being unfair to him. All he had really done was kiss his partner and I couldn't tell whether I was bothered by that or by the way he had done it.

After breakfast, I drove the boys back to town and to their motel. The ride in the Jeep was quiet, ending with a polite handshake from Robert and an unexpected and warm embrace from David.

SIX

ALTHOUGH I WAS ITCHY and eager to get home, my reaction to visiting town so many times in so few days, I decided to stop by Myra's and pick up shots for the young coyote. I considered it ironic that if left in the wild she would have been healthy, contact with humans notwithstanding, but because she was in our care she now had to be protected from distemper, parvo, and a host of other things. Protection against rabies would come later. The thought of rabies reminded me of my primary concern, that the little dog was a wild animal. Normally, I could see raising her in a cage and then turning her free to roam and hunt, but this pathetic creature had but three legs and who knew what kind of respiratory damage she might have suffered. I'd have to establish our respective stations and socialize her as best I could.

As I drove back through town, the medicine in a shoe box with dry ice around it, I considered Gus's attachment to the coyote. It seemed a bit extreme, but the pup was plenty pitiful. What little traffic there was slowed near the square. I could see an ambulance parked in front of the sheriff's office. I inched closer and I saw a stretcher being rolled along the walk to the vehicle. Bucky was standing nearby, his hat in his hand while he scratched his equine head. I tapped my horn and the tall man turned to see me. He walked to my rig.

"What's going on, Bucky?" I asked.

He put a hand on the roof of the Jeep and leaned toward me. He spat on the ground before saying, "It's bad, John."

"What?"

"Your friend killed himself," Bucky said.

"Castlebury?"

"Hanged himself from the upper bunk with his britches. One leg around his neck, the other around the top rail. I sure didn't see it coming. Should have."

"Good grief."

"Terrible thing to see." The sheriff looked over at the ambulance doors being slammed shut. "Terrible thing."

"Good grief," I said, again.

Bucky stood and looked away across the lawn of the courthouse. "It's about the last thing I need, I can tell you that." Then he fell silent.

"What is it, Bucky?" I asked.

"Nothing."

"You don't think he did it," I said.

"What do you think?" he asked. The ambulance drove away, no siren. "You knew him a little."

"No, I don't think he did it." I was surprised to have said it, but I knew I'd thought it all along. "You still haven't told me what you think."

"I don't know, John. It's felt funny from the beginning to me."

"So, what now?" I asked.

"I guess I'll do my job. Now, I guess I'll get around to doing my fucking job." He shook his head. "We both know I'll never find out who killed that boy. Jesus Christ. Two men dead."

I nodded. "I'll make the call for you."

Bucky looked at me.

"I know you," I said. "You look for your murderer. I'll call Castlebury's brother."

"Thanks. Still, you're going to have to tell him to call my office."

Bucky stood away and I drove off. Bucky had a hard time with bad news, an obvious liability in his profession. He was either tender that way, and if true, I liked that, or he was weak. But I wondered why I was not either tender or weak. Fact was, I had little stomach for it as well, and I wondered why in the world I had offered to do it.

Perhaps I thought I owed something to Wallace Castlebury. Perhaps I felt I'd failed to let him think that at least one person thought he was innocent. Maybe he'd have been alive if he thought I believed him. I carried enough guilt and I wasn't going to carry any more. I would call his brother and do this last thing for him.

At home, I put the shots for the dog in the medicine refrigerator in the tack room. I then walked across the yard toward the house. All the snow was gone, but somehow I could tell that it had been there. I stepped into the kitchen to find Gus nursing a cup of tea.

He put down his cup and tilted his head like a dog. "So, what's wrong?" he asked.

"Wallace Castlebury hanged himself."

Gus whistled, picked up his cup and sipped some tea. He looked down at the pup on the blanket by his feet. "Such is life." He leaned over, put his hand down and the little coyote pushed toward him. "She's stronger."

"I see."

"You realize we haven't named her."

"That's your job," I said.

"What about Spirit?" he said.

"Sure, if that's what you want hippie-Jim."

"Just fooling around," he said. He stroked the little head. "Her name is Isosceles. Maybe Tripod. Maybe Nubby."

"I suppose any of those will work, Gus," I said. I studied my uncle for a few seconds. "Hey, Gus, you feeling all right?"

"Fine. Why?"

"Just asking."

Susie had for a time accused me of being interested in a young woman who had brought her three-year-old Arabian mare to me for training. That was how she had put it. "You're interested in her," she would say. I laughed it off every time. "Don't you think she's beautiful?" Susie asked once.

"What's that got to do with anything?" I asked back. "You're beautiful and I happen to be married to you."

"You didn't answer my question," she said.

"Question?"

"Do you think she's beautiful?"

"She's attractive. Lots of people are attractive."

"And you like her," Susie said.

"I don't like the way this is going," I said. "Why don't you just tell me what's eating at you? She's a kid. Listen, I'm not interested in anyone but you. It never occurred to me to think of her as attractive until you mentioned it."

"So, you do find her attractive."

"I love you, Susie. You're my life."

She claimed to be satisfied and to have let the matter go, but still a distance had been created and she was, at least that night, cool to the touch. I told her I loved her and went to sleep with my hand on her hip.

A few days later, the young woman, Lane, was at my place for a lesson on her horse. I was standing in the middle of the round pen, watching, asking her to position her arms in various ways. She was a tough, lean woman who wanted badly to conquer her fear of horses, particularly this big and unruly horse. I didn't have the horse on a line, not that that would have helped. Something got into the mare and she kicked out and bucked her way across the midpoint of the circle, namely me. Lane began to lose her balance and I stepped to the horse and righted her. She was shaken a little and I helped her down. Our faces were close and I realized in that moment that Susie had been correct; I no doubt knew all along that she was right, but I was being defensive and, basically, male. Lane and I kissed. A brief kiss, but a kiss nonetheless. I kicked the dirt like an idiot and did the only thing that seemed decent, I said I was sorry and looked at the horse. Nothing else happened.

Later that day, no doubt to prove beyond any doubt that I was an idiot, I confessed to Susie that I had kissed Lane. I did it to make myself feel better, I realized later; that could have been my only reason. I thought I had been a bad man, a bad husband, and I believed that being forthright and honest would fix me up. I was a selfish jerk and some part of me must have wanted to hurt Susie. That's all I can imagine. I really wasn't then a stupid man, but I was, apparently, an idiot. The reaction was what any reasonable person would expect and I don't think we ever really got over it. All of my apologies never offered a why. I didn't have any whys to offer.

It was odd to be thinking of Susie while I prepared to call Wallace Castlebury's brother. I was sitting in my study, looking out the window at the hills. There were no clouds collected over them; that was good. It was a beautiful day. I didn't procrastinate, didn't find a leaky faucet to repair, didn't clean my already-too-clean rifle. I picked up the phone and pushed in the number.

I identified myself and the man on the other end said, "What is it?" But his tone was different this time, perhaps softer, perhaps he was just tired.

"I'm sorry," I said. "I've got bad news. I've been asked to notify you that your brother is dead."

"Dead?"

"I'm sorry." I was surprised to detect a note of sadness, given the tone and content of our last conversation. "He killed himself." I thought to spare even this uncaring relative the grizzly details of his brother's death. In fact, I was sure at that moment that I had agreed to make the call only because I believed the man would be unmoved by the news. So much for what I thought I knew.

"What?" the man said. "My brother is dead?" I could hear that he was beginning to weep.

"Is this Wallace Castlebury's brother?" I was suddenly terrified that I had misled another man into believing his brother was dead.

"Oh, lord, poor Wallace," he cried. "Poor, poor Wallace."

I don't think I was ever so confused in my life. I looked out the window that faced the barn and saw the mule emerge.

"How did he die?"

"He killed himself. If you want details, you'll have to call the

Highland sheriff's office." I gave him the number. "In fact, you're supposed to call there anyway. About the body and all."

"The body," the man wailed.

"How did he kill himself?"

"I don't think I'm supposed to say any more," I said. "I'm sorry for your loss and I'm sorry to have had to give you such news."

"Brother," he said. "I have found the Lord Jesus Christ and brought him into my life just last week. I'm saved now and I'd like you to pray with me for my poor, poor brother, Wallace. Do you know if he found God before his death?"

"I have no idea."

"Pray with me," he said.

"I think you should call the sheriff's office. Here's that number again." I read it off.

"Dear Jesus," he said, as if dictating a letter. "Please find the soul of my poor lost brother and guide him into your sweet, forgiving arms. Open those beautiful gates of that beautiful heaven to him in spite of his sick and evil doings, his homosexualness and his short-comings." He wept loudly. "And help me stay away from the sub-stances, you know the ones I mean, so that I might serve you better. In your name, Jesus-God-Almighty, amen."

"Okay, one more time, here's that number." I gave him the num-ber one last time and hung up. I was exhausted. I felt as though I had been chased by a cougar.

I picked up the phone again. This time I called Morgan and in-vited her over for a ride into the desert. She seemed puzzled by the quality of my invitation and so I said, "I think I need some company and I don't think Gus is it." Thinking that was not exactly romantic, I added, "And I'd really like to see you. I'd like to try that kissing thing one more time. If that's okay."

She said she'd think about it, but we could certainly go for a ride.

The sun didn't have to compete with any clouds and so my jacket was off and stuffed into my saddlebag. I rode Felony and I put Morgan on my Appaloosa. She hadn't trailered her horse to my place for fear that there might still be some icy patches on the highway. My mare needed the exercise anyway. We rode up high and got really cold. Morgan asked me about the cave.

"It's not far from here," I told her.

"Care to show me?"

"I don't know." Felony snorted and stepped uneasy and I knew he was feeling my tension. I slowed my breathing and he went off the muscle. "Why do you want to go there?" I asked.

"I'm just curious to see it."

"We don't have flashlights," I said.

"I just want to see where the damn cave is, John. But if you don't want to show me . . ."

"That's not it." I wheeled Felony about on his haunches. "Come on, let's go. Over the ridge and facing the desert."

On the way, she said, "It's bad about that Castlebury."

I agreed.

"I don't want to talk or think about him, though."

"Why do you say that?" I asked.

"I know you're thinking about him."

"A little," I said.

"Well, I don't want to."

"Okay," I said. "What do you want to think about?"

"Us," she said.

"I can do that."

"See to it then," she said. She laughed then kicked the mare and trotted away from me. Morgan was right about most things, mainly because she was patient. She'd been patient with me, that was for sure. She was smart and she lived hard.

At the entrance to the cave, we dismounted. I tied Felony by wedging a knot between two boulders. The App would stand on a dropped rein. We walked inside several yards.

"Wow," Morgan said. "This really is a cave."

"It stays this big for a while, then it branches a couple times. One of the branches opens into quite a large cavern. I've found only one tight spot. Tight for me anyway. I haven't gone through it yet."

"You are getting a little chunky there." Morgan poked her index finger at my belt buckle.

"Watch out, sister," I said. I caught her hand and pulled her to me. I felt excited and stupid. I kicked myself inside, realizing that any thoughts of Susie now were indulgent and convenient. I toyed with the lie that I was afraid of hurting her, so I kicked myself again. I looked at her eyes. "You understand, of course, that I'm basically stupid."

"I noticed that right away."

"I also have very strong feelings for you, ma'am."

"So, you're not completely stupid."

"Apparently not." I leaned forward and put my lips on Morgan's. I closed my eyes this time. I pulled back. "Thank you, ma'am."

"Anytime."

"So, let's get out of here."

Morgan shook her head and looked back into the cave. "Let's go in a little deeper."

"We don't have a light," I told her.

"So what?"

"Okay, let's go."

We walked in about thirty yards and made the first bend. Once around it, everything was pitch dark.

"Jesus," Morgan said. "I've never seen it so dark."

"That's a funny way to put it."

"So, why don't we try that kiss again?" she asked.

I felt her breath on my chin as I reached around her. She was different in the complete dark, but I could still feel the beauty of her face. We kissed again, this time more urgently. This time I felt my lips soften more to hers. I touched her face. Morgan put her hand between us, placed her palm flat against my chest, then brushed down my body to below my belt. She put her open hand against my penis and pressed into me. I kissed her harder, finding the tip of her tongue with mine. I thought to be afraid, to become shy, but I let that go, smelling her hair in the dark, feeling the warmth of her breath on my ear and neck. I opened her jacket and shirt and touched her breasts. I thought that they seemed smaller in the dark and I liked that. I ran my hands up and around her neck, loving the heat of her skin. In the dark we were clumsy with our clothes, but we got them off, enough of them off, and Morgan and I made love, my backside on my jacket on the cool floor of the cave, she sitting on me. We didn't say anything, but I listened to every sound she made, every breath she let out, every click she made with her fingernails. The fingernail clicking, a nervous action between thumb and fore-finger I had witnessed before, in the light, when she was thinking. And behind that sound was the forever-there dripping of the cave's water. When she came, at least I thought she came, a wave of fear like none I'd felt in a long while washed over me, made me shudder. I guess to her it felt like I had come. We stopped moving and lay there, her palms flat against my chest, my hands on her waist.

"I love you, John," she said.

And in the dark there, I told her the truth, the whole scary truth. I said, "I love you, too."

Finding our clothes in the dark was considerably more difficult than removing them had been. It wasn't until we were back in the light that we could see what we had done. Both our shirts were in-correctly buttoned and I found myself squirming, then realized that my underwear was on backwards. Morgan watched while I stripped down to get things straight. I began to feel self-conscious, which was fairly dumb, given what we'd just done.

"Are you feeling shy?" she asked.

"No, why?"

"You're covering up."

"I am not."

"You most certainly are," she said.

I faced her. "I am not."

"Mr. Hunt," she sighed.

Then I covered up. "Okay, okay," I said, pulling on my clothes. "So, I'm shy. What do you want from me?"

"Exactly this," she said and kissed me while I buckled my belt.

The ride back was easier than I had imagined all those days before. We were relaxed, talking, laughing, and so Felony rode better than ever. We cantered across a meadow and then walked, letting the horses catch their breath.

"You're good for me, young lady," I said.

"Why do you say that, you old fart?"

"You're good for this nutty horse, too."

"So, you think we'll ever do that again?" Morgan asked.

I looked at her and realized she was joking. "I suppose. Once or twice more, the events being judiciously spaced so we don't become bored."

"So, when were you thinking the next time might be?"

"Couple hours from now."

We loosened the girths and walked the horses the last quarter-mile home. We didn't speak, but it felt right. Morgan had to go home and see to Emily, and so I took the horses and got them squared away. When I walked into the house, Gus smiled at me, stared, and smiled some more.

"What's with you?" I asked.

"Me?"

"Yeah, you?" I said.

"You had sex, didn't you?"

"What?" I was embarrassed.

"It's all over you." Then I made the mistake of looking all over me. "What are you talking about?"

"You had sex."

"You're a dirty old man," I said.

"There's nothing to be ashamed of," he said. "I was beginning to think there was something wrong with you. Prostate-wise or something."

"No, apparently I'm okay."

"Glad to hear it."

"You're not going to say anything to Emily, are you?"

"You think I'm a damn fool?" he asked.

"Now that you mention it."

"We're having what you call locker-room talk," he said.

"That's what you're having. I'll be in the other room."

"I'm happy for you," Gus said and turned toward the kitchen.

SEVEN

I WAS DEEPER into the cave than I had ever been. I had taken a bag of chalk with me and was marking my trail as I went. My light found it easily and I felt more secure than ever. Without traffic from animals, I also felt confident that my powder markers would remain undisturbed. I made my way across the big room to another opening and pushed myself about three hundred yards deeper. The darkness was heavy, sweet, and thick, and it scared me more than a little. I squeezed through a tight spot, two walls of rock formed a twenty-foot-high, nine-inch-wide chimney. I promised myself to shed a few pounds once I had popped through and was looking at it from the other side. Looking at the "fat man's misery," I wondered if, in fact, I would be able to squeeze my fat behind back through. I recalled when a child got his head stuck between banister spindles and everyone was wondering how he got it through in the first place. My heart began to race and I reminded myself that I was panicking before I had reason to. I pushed my arm into the crack, then my shoulder. Then, turning to face my direction of travel, I pushed my head into the crevice. The space felt even tighter now. I was convinced that I was swelling with uncertainty. I inhaled my gut in and my hips. I inch-wormed my way through and popped out like a cork. I couldn't help laughing. The feeling was exquisite, not only the feeling of freedom from the cramped place, but from the fear itself. I looked back at the crack, my headlamp illuminating it, dark all around and dark in its core.

After the squeeze, the rest of the cave felt a bit more comfortable, familiar. Then, about a hundred yards from the cave's mouth, my hand-held light flashed over something. I came back with the beam and after a few sweeps found it. It was a bit of paper and some dried brown shreds. I put the shreds of dried leaves to my nose and, though I could not detect an odor, I realized it was tobacco. It had been the butt of a cigarette and it had been field stripped, the paper opened up and the tobacco shaken free, an act meant to avoid detection, for some a mere habit. Fear washed over me, but a different kind a of fear this time. This time it was real fear, the kind that no place, no storm, no animal can make, only humans. It could have been there for years, I told myself. In the dark here, I certainly had not seen everything. In fact, I marveled every visit at how much was new to me. It could have been there for forty years, a Shoshone veteran of the Korean War looking for a quiet place, or a soldier from a hundred years ago. And as I looked at the tiny bit of paper, I realized it could have been left there hours ago.

It was midday and I was driving through town on my way to the reservation. Daniel White Buffalo had called and left a message with Gus that he really wanted me to come over to his place. His ranch was on the edge of the reservation. He had good water and this rankled a lot of the white ranchers around him; they were even less pleased when he increased his place by buying adjacent, nontribal land. Gus hadn't picked up any details on the phone, but he thought White Buffalo had said something about somebody or something being shot. I turned off the highway and down the road toward the ranch. I looked across the big pasture and saw a sheriff's rig parked near the house. I gave the Jeep a little more gas and kicked up some dust getting there. Bucky, Hanks, and Daniel White Buffalo turned and watched me get out and walk toward them. The stocky Arapaho man shook my hand and said he was glad I came. He ran a nervous hand over his hair and stopped at the knot of his braid.

"Who called you?" Bucky asked.

"Daniel did," I said.

"Yeah, I called him," Daniel said. "John's got good sense. So do you, Bucky, but John, he's like family."

I thought this was odd since I seldom saw the man. I'd trained a couple horses for him and it was his mule that was haunting my barns.

"What's going on?" I asked.

"Somebody shot a cow," Hanks said with a slightly dismissive tone.

"Shooting a cow is a big deal," Daniel said. "That's two thousand dollars lying in that gulley."

"Let's go have a look," Bucky said.

We piled into Daniel's open-topped late-sixties Bronco and bounced across the pasture and toward the creek. He'd called Bucky because the cow was shot off the reservation, in the county, Bucky's jurisdiction. I didn't know why he'd called me. He came to an abrupt halt that we were all expecting, but still sent us lurching forward.

The cow was lying about ten yards up the opposite creek bank. I sloshed through the water to the animal. He'd been shot through the head. Just beneath the ear. I looked back to see Bucky and Hanks picking their way over the rocks.

"Shot, all right," I reported.

Hanks turned back to see Daniel White Buffalo leaning against his truck. "What are you doing over there?" he called.

"I've seen him," Daniel said. "My getting wet again won't change his condition much."

Bucky folded his long frame to a knee beside me. "So, what am I supposed to do?" he asked.

"You got me," I said. "He's been shot. There's no denying that."

"I suppose I can get a vet to dig the slug out of his brain and try to match it up to one of the eight million guns in this county."

"He was shot pretty close up," I said. "Pretty messy." I stood and walked upstream some yards, then up the bank. I spotted a beer can and beside it a place on the ground where someone had lost his footing. "Looks like he had a picnic," I said.

Hanks started toward me. He turned back to the sheriff and said, "At least if the vet dug out the slug we'd know the caliber."

"I'd say it was a two-twenty-three," I said.

"And how would you know that?" Hanks asked.

"Shell casing," I said. I held it up on the end of a stick.

Bucky gave me a look, a different look than he would have given me if I'd said thirty-thirty or forty-five.

Hanks picked up the can. "Pabst," he said. "Still has beer in it. Whoever it was will drink anything, that's for damn sure."

Bucky shook his head. "Hanks, are you holding that can in your hand?"

Hanks dropped it. Beer spilled out and made a rivulet down the slope into the stream.

"Well, pick it up again, with a stick this time, and put it in an evidence bag. Maybe we can still get a print off the damn thing. As if that will do us a damn bit of good."

"I'm sorry, Sheriff," Hanks said. The deputy collected the can and the casing in separate plastic bags.

We walked back across the creek to Daniel White Buffalo.

"He's still dead," Bucky said.

"I thought so," Daniel said.

Bucky looked back at the cow, then at the sky. "I hear that you were complaining in town about Clara Monday stealing your cattle."

"Yeah, I've been thinking that for a while," Daniel said. "I've lost a couple beefs and I've seen her up on the ridge riding that horse. Spooky. Old lady riding around on a horse like that."

"You think she might have done this?"

Daniel laughed. "I believe in my heart that she's a rustler, but she sure as hell ain't wasteful."

That seemed to satisfy Bucky. "Well, that's about all there is to see and do here. Let's go back."

"Who do you think did it?" I asked Daniel as I climbed into the passenger seat beside him.

"I don't know. I have absolutely no idea."

When we arrived back at the house, Hanks jumped out quickly and Bucky worked himself free.

"I'll give you a call, White Buffalo," Bucky said.

"Yeah, right," Daniel said, more to the ground than to them.

Daniel walked slowly to my Jeep. "Sorry about the beef," I told Daniel. "Scary stuff."

"You got that right."

We tossed absent waves to Bucky and the deputy as they rolled away toward the road.

"Speaking of scary stuff, when are you going to come pick up that mule of yours? He keeps escaping."

"He's yours."

"He's a nice ride now," I told him. "But I don't need a mule."

"Indians don't get on with mules," Daniel said.

"Don't give me that shit."

"You ever see an Indian riding a mule? Not even in the movies." Daniel gestured to his place with a sweep of his hand. "It's nice here, and why? No mule."

"Not so nice," I said.

Daniel remembered the cow, too. "Not so nice," he repeated.

"Why did you call me anyway?" I asked.

"I wanted a witness here for the sheriff, so he could see somebody seeing him."

"You don't trust Bucky?"

Daniel shook his head, then pulled out a cigarette, lit it. "I trust him about as much as I trust any white man with a gun."

"Yeah, well, sorry about the cow."

As I backed up to turn around, Daniel said, "Enjoy that mule."

I stopped and pulled forward, close to him. "You understand that you owe me for his board and food."

"How much?"

"Near five hundred dollars."

Daniel whistled.

"What happens if I don't pay?" he asked.

"Well, the law says, he's mine to sell."

"Have at it, buckaroo."

I drove away. I'd been taken advantage of, but I wasn't too upset. If I had a mind to, I could sell the beast for twelve, fifteen hundred. But I didn't have a mind to. I actually liked having him around.

On Thanksgiving morning Morgan's mother died. I was trimming hooves when Gus called to me from the house end of the barn. "Phone," was all he said. I found myself trotting, then sprinting. Gus said, "Morgan," as he trotted behind me. My messy boots slipped on the linoleum as I crossed to the phone.

"Morgan?"

"It's mother." She was crying. "She won't wake up. I've called nine-one-one."

"I'm on my way."

On the phone with the emergency operator, Morgan had used the magic words "heart attack." And so the medivac helicopter was already there when I arrived. The blades were still turning and the horses in the pasture were tearing around through the wet grass and mud. The sky was bright blue and the yellow helicopter set against it made the scene surreal. Emily was being carried to the open craft as I climbed out. Morgan ran to me and I held her, but she didn't need to be held. She told me that the paramedics would not let her ride in the helicopter with Emily.

"I'm driving you to town," I said. "Get in."

I opened the passenger side and got her in. Suddenly she was like an elk caught in a bright light. I buckled her belt and closed the door. As I drove away from the house she stared ahead through the windshield.

"I knew she wasn't right this morning," she finally said. "I asked her, I said, 'Are you okay?' and she waved me off. Oh, god. I knew it. I just knew something was wrong."

I put my hand on her leg. I considered a list of platitudes, but

they all seemed unusable. Years ago, I had often felt ambushed by
Susie when bad things happened. I would offer a quiet hand of support and she would ask why I wasn't saying anything. Then I'd say
something, admittedly vacuous but meant in the spirit of support,
and she would snap at me, asking what that was supposed to mean
or accusing me of belittling her fear or grief. Now, I remained silent
and if Morgan asked me to speak, I planned to say, "I'm right here."

"Do you think she's going to die?" she asked.

"I don't know," I said, realizing that 'I'm here for you' wasn't going
to work.

"She was so limp. Maybe she was already dead."

I squeezed her thigh.

"John."

"Yes?"

"I love you," she said.

"I love you, too, honey." We made the big curve around the mountain. "Twenty minutes," I said.

"Twenty minutes?"

"To town."

"Twenty minutes to town." Morgan closed her eyes and let her
head rest against the seat.

When we arrived, the helicopter was idle on its pad, and a nurse
was watching through the emergency-room doors. Morgan looked
at me and I pulled her close. We walked to the hospital, knowing already that Emily was gone.

Emily had been laid on a bed in a curtained stall. Her face still
looked alive, with some color in her cheeks. A sheet was pulled up to
her shoulders. Her hair was wild about her head and Morgan sought
to straighten it. The doctor stood there with Morgan and talked to
her. I stood there, feeling sad and sick and weak. I thought of the el-
derly person I had left at my house. I stepped into the hall and used
the phone at the nurse's station to call Gus. After I gave him the
news there was a long silence.

"Gus?"

"I'm here."

"You okay?"

"Fine."

"I'll feed. You stay with Morgan."

"Thanks, Gus."

I arranged for the one mortuary in Highland to come for Emily while Morgan took care of matters with the hospital. I then drove her home. I wanted to take her to my place, but she insisted. I got a fire going while she straightened up. Emily had fallen in the den and things had been left disturbed.

"It's cold in here," Morgan said.

It wasn't cold, but I said, "I'll have the fire good and hot shortly."

"She just fell over, John." Morgan was standing in front of the sofa. "She didn't make a sound. I didn't see her face. I don't think she felt anything. The doctor said she probably didn't feel anything. He said her heart probably just stopped."

I walked to her and lowered her to the sofa. I sat beside her with my arm around her.

"Do you think she went peacefully?" Morgan asked me.

"I do," I said.

Morgan didn't cry, but she fell fast asleep quickly. I untwisted our bodies and went outside to feed her horses and check the gates. I came back into the house and called Gus. He took a long time answering and I started to get upset. He picked up.

"Everything okay?" I asked.

"All is fine," he said.

"What took you so long?"

"I was busy, do you mind?"

I caught myself, caught my worry and caught the anxiety that had been working on me. "I'm sorry, Gus."

"How's Morgan?"

"She's asleep."

"I've got things covered here."

"Okay."

"Get some sleep," he said. "I mean it."

"Yes, sir."

I didn't wake Morgan, but let her sleep the night on the sofa. I sat nearby in a stuffed chair and watched her, realizing with each sleep-breath she took that I did, in fact, love her. And I didn't love her because I needed to love someone, but because she wouldn't go away, not physically, but in my head.

Morning came and Morgan was still asleep. I went out into the clear crisp air to feed the animals. I put the hay in the feeder in the pasture and noticed Morgan's horse, Square, arching her neck and coughing. It was an odd behavior, but she went for her food. She wanted to eat, so I didn't think she was about to colic. Then she arched again and I thought she might be choking, which seemed odd since she hadn't eaten anything yet. Choking on hay is uncommon and choking on the green grass is really uncommon. I haltered her and removed her from the food. I put her in a paddock and made sure there was water for her. Morgan came from the house in a thick robe, her face already worried.

"What's going on?" she asked.

"Square's acting funny," I said.

"What's wrong?"

"I don't know if there's anything wrong yet."

Just then the horse arched her neck again and coughed.

"What was that?" Morgan asked.

"That's the funny thing," I said.

"What's wrong with her, John?" Everything was piling up on poor Morgan. She started to cry. Since there's nothing wrong with crying, I didn't get in her way. I simply proceeded with what I had to do with the horse. "Go to my truck and bring me my red box. I've got a speculum in there."

She trotted, the robe trailing behind her, crying there and back.

I had my thumbs in the horse's cheeks and was trying to see into her throat, trying to spot any kind of obstruction. "I need a flashlight," I said. "There's a penlight in the jockey box."

She ran crying to get it. She came back and I asked her to hold the lead rope while I looked. I held the light in my teeth and opened Square's mouth again. I grabbed her tongue and pulled it to the side. She was drooling and I saw that there was a bit of blood mixed in it. I saw a wire or a stick in her throat.

"Yep," I said.

"What is it?" Morgan asked.

"She's got something in there all right."

"Oh, my god," she said.

"She's okay, Morgan."

"Can you get it out?"

"I'm going to try." I didn't want to tell her that if I couldn't we were going to have to take her to the clinic down in Laramie and have the vet knock her out and find a way to get it out. I just couldn't bring myself to tell her that. "It's not too far back there."

"John?"

"Okay, I'm going to give her some butte; that will make her feel better. I've got one shot of that left right here. And I'm going to sedate her slightly as well, but you're going to have to hold her. Okay?"

"Okay." Tears were streaming down Morgan's face now.

I gave the horse the shots. Morgan watched as I found the vein, pulled a little blood into the syringe, then pumped the drug into the horse. In just a few minutes, Square's head was hanging low.

"Is she all right?" Morgan asked.

"High as a kite," I said. "Come and stand over on this side." I took the rope and let Morgan walk around me to the right side of the horse. I set the speculum in Square's mouth, essentially a piece of metal to wedge between the horse's back teeth, and said, "Morgan, you're going to have to hold this right here for me, okay, honey?"

She nodded, taking the metal tee of a handle and bracing it against the nose band of the halter.

"Oh, John, what if you can't get it out?"

I didn't say anything at first and then I thought that my silence might alarm her more. "This thing, whatever it is, is probably just sticking up through her soft palate. Shouldn't be a problem." Of course I didn't know that at all. The horse began doing what horses do and that was chewing. At least she was trying to chew; the coil of metal of the speculum was in her way. But she was chewing enough that she was catching my knuckles. It hurt like hell, but I had to get the thing out. I couldn't let this crush Morgan. Instead, my hand was getting crushed. I grabbed the object and it poked me; it had thorns. I didn't pull back. I was in there now. I grabbed it, a thorn piercing my thumb, and I worked it free and slowly pulled it out. I held it out for Morgan to see. It was a four-inch-long wishbone of a rose twig.

"That's it?" she said.

"That's it."

Morgan looked at my bleeding knuckle and my bleeding thumb. "Your hand," she said.

"It's okay."

I was about to tell her I was all right, to take the horse back and not worry about me, but I was proud that I made a good decision for once, a selfless and right decision, a smart one. I let my friend take care of me. I let her look at the damage, wash me and bandage me and it was good. I let her take care of me and it was right.

I drove to town to pick up butte powder for Morgan's horse and more for my supplies as well. I needed other things and tried to remember as best I could. Gus had told me to go take care of that and to pick up some groceries and a paper, too. He could feel, I imagined, that I was starting to worry about him and he was essentially kicking me out of the house until I came to my senses.

At the feed store, Myra was shaking her head. "Emily," she said. "I thought she'd live forever. I thought she and old Clara Monday up on the reservation would never go. But I guess everybody does."

"Sounds right," I said.

"How's Morgan?" she asked.

"It's hard."

"It always is," Myra said. She looked at my stuff on the counter. "Let's call it fifty even."

"Okay."

"You tell Morgan she can call me if she wants to talk. I lost my mother just last year."

"Myra, I didn't know. I'll tell her."

I walked out of the store and I guess I was looking down or not looking at all because I bumped into somebody. I excused myself and then saw the skinny face of one of the men who had fought with David and Robert. I remembered him immediately. The face of his partner was close behind him.

"Watch yourself, nigger," the man said.

I'm a grown man with more than my share of self-control, so I ignored him and moved toward my Jeep.

"I said, watch yourself, nigger," he repeated and gave me an open-handed shove in the shoulder.

I didn't bother explaining to the malformed creature that he had chosen the wrong man on the wrong day to say the wrong thing. If I had, he might not have been so surprised by the quick left that started in my middle and launched from a coil that had been tightening for years. The bandage on my hand became red again, but not with my blood this time as the idiot's nose exploded under my punch. The man's apish friend took a dash at me, but I guess it was the look in my red eyes or the recocking of my bloody fist that stopped him. The bigger man examined his friend's face, then renewed his resolve and glared at me.

I readjusted my package under my right arm. "And I kinda liked him," I said and didn't move away.

He looked back to the bloody face.

I walked to my rig and drove off to the grocery market, feeling bad and good, relieved and soiled.

I wouldn't tell Gus about the confrontation. At best, the story would have reaffirmed his suspicion of this part of the country and, at worst, he would have wanted to drive into town and find the bastards. I was putting the food away when he came downstairs into the kitchen.

"How's Morgan?" he asked.

"Good."

He let out a soft whistle and from the blanket the little coyote dragged herself across the floor toward him, almost balancing on her three legs, almost hopping. Her little face was open and panting.

"How about that," I said.

"Something, eh?"

I nodded.

"I've named her."

"Again? I thought her name was Spirit or some such thing."

"Her name is Emily. Do you think Morgan will mind? I mean I'm not going to tell her today."

I watched Gus go to his knee and give the puppy a scratch. "I don't think she'll mind at all, Gus. I think she'll like it."

"By the way, that mule is out."

"Well, of course he is," I said.

"Been out better part of the day."

"He's going to have to stay out. I can't be fussing with that fool animal tonight. I'm going to feed and then go over to Morgan's."

"Good. I'll make a dinner plate for her." Gus gained his feet and walked over to the refrigerator. "And I don't want you rushing back in the morning. I can feed everybody here and if I go out there and find a horse with an extra leg or a bear in the tack room, I'll call you."

Emily's funeral was a quiet affair. She had not been particularly religious during her life and no one saw fit to impose that on her now. A couple hundred people showed up at the Lutheran church where the Lutheran minister apologized for being a minister and mentioned a couple of nice things about the deceased, among them the fact that she had once repeatedly hauled her stock trailer up a burning mountain to rescue horses and the fact that she had come to sit with his own dying wife years ago. The minister said, "Emily didn't express or show objection to my praying by my wife's bedside and I won't insult her beliefs by praying now." Everyone mumbled agreement and the service was over in fifteen minutes.

"Now, that's a funeral," Gus said.

There was no graveside ceremony. Emily would be cremated and her ashes picked up by Morgan on Thursday. On that Monday, about fifty people gathered at Morgan's house and ate food they had brought and more or less got in the way, hanging about in changing clusters in the kitchen, living room, and in the yard.

Duncan Camp and I stood on the porch and looked out over the pasture. I told him about Square's twig.

"Horses," he said. "Suicidal bastards, every one. You're lucky it stopped in the front like that. And that she didn't gnaw your finger off."

"You got that right."

He took a long, deep breath. "You think Morgan will do okay here alone?" Duncan asked. "This is a big place."

"She'll do fine."

"I guess so. She and the old lady held it down pretty good."

"They did," I said.

"Well, we'll check on her, won't we?"

I nodded.

Myra came outside, screen door smacking shut behind her. She pulled her sweater tight against the chilly air. "John, Morgan went upstairs. She asked me to find you and tell you to get your ass up there."

"She put it like that, did she?"

"No, I added the emphasis."

"Well done." I excused myself and went inside. I climbed the stairs and found Morgan in Emily's room, standing at the open closet.

"So, what's going on?" I asked.

She took an armful of clothes on hangers from the rod and tossed them onto the bed.

"Cleaning out already?" I asked.

"My mother's voice is pretty clear in my head. 'If it's cold you build a fire, if it's hot you jump in a creek. Life's simple like that.' She was right. My mother's dead. That's a simple fact. Life continues. That's how she'd want me to think. And that's how I'm going to think." She looked out the window at the barn below. "John, thank you."

"You bet. What would you like me to do? I mean, can I help in here?"

Morgan sat on the bed, rubbed her open hand on the bedspread. "There are some empty boxes in the tack room. Would you run out and get them?"

"Of course I will. What about all those people downstairs?" I asked. "You want me to tell them anything?"

"They'll be fine. And I'm fine. You know that, don't you, John?"

"I know." I walked to the door. "You want anything else?"

"Bring us up a bottle of wine and some glasses. Two bottles."

EIGHT

THE MORNING was hard cold. I'd just come in from breaking the ice on the horses' water. I was heating water for tea and looking out at the foot of snow that covered the ground. The snow was still falling and every half-hour or so I would go out and sweep the steps. Emily, the little coyote, skated around on the linoleum of the kitchen while Zoe watched from the corner. The older dog's interest in the puppy had diminished some, but she still kept an eye on her. Out the window, the sun was just reaching the top of the barn.

"Good morning," Gus said as he came into the room.

"Morning, Gus."

"And how's my little girl?" he cooed to the pup. He reached down and let the coyote chew on his finger."

"Gus, I don't think you should do that," I said.

"Oh, yeah, right."

"I'd like you to flip her on her back as often as you think of it. Hold her there until she doesn't struggle."

"Okay."

"This is important, Gus."

"I hear you," he said.

"I'm sorry." I grabbed the kettle and poured my tea water. "I don't mean to be a nag." But I did.

"Where's Morgan?" Gus asked.

"I think she's still sleeping. That's how I left her anyway. It's a good morning to sleep."

Gus looked out the window over the sink. "Christmas Eve already. Is it as cold at it looks out there?"

"Oh, yeah. It hasn't been this cold since the last time it was this cold." I sat at the table with my mug.

"You mean yesterday."

I nodded. "Hey, how about whipping up some of those farm fresh eggs and that fake bacon?"

"Sure thing." He went to the refrigerator and took eggs from the tray in the door. "How do you want them? Scrambled, over-easy, sunny-side-up, hard-boiled, soft-boiled, poached, or shirred?"

"Surprise me." I got up and put my mug in the sink. "I'm going up to see my sweetie."

"I'll take my time," he said.

I walked up the stairs, trying to avoid the squeaky spots and stood in the doorway, watched Morgan sleep. She was facing me and the light through the window was falling over her covered legs.

"Hey there, cowboy, why aren't you in the bed with me?" she asked in a sleepy voice.

"For one thing, I'm wearing filthy clothes and for another, I think you'd find my hands to be freezing cold."

"I don't care," she said. "I can take it."

"Well, okay then." I kicked off my house shoes, pulled back the covers, and crawled in beside her. When my hands hit her warm skin, she screamed. "I told you they were cold."

"Get those icy things off me."

"You said you could take it." I put my knuckles on her stomach. "How's that? Cold enough?"

She let out a shriek, slapped at my hands. "No, not there, not there. Put them on my butt, on my butt."

I did as instructed. "Is that okay?"

"Yes. Actually, that's not bad," she said.

"Not bad? Whatever happened to 'great' or 'good'?" I made to go again for her belly.

"Good, good," she said. "That feels good. Please, please, please don't touch my stomach."

I pulled my hands back and looked at the ceiling. "Gus is making breakfast. Eggs and that awful phony bacon."

"Do I have time to shower?"

"I insist," I said.

"Wise guy." Morgan kissed me, then pushed me down as she climbed over me and out of the bed. "I'll be right down." She was pulling off her nightshirt as she walked into the bathroom.

"Who wears a nightshirt these days?" I asked. I followed her and leaned on the sink, watched her step into the shower.

"Old-fashioned girls like me," she said. She turned on the water and stood away from the spray while she checked the temperature.

"Hey, old-fashioned girl."

She talked over the sound of the water, stepping into it now. "Yes? What do you want to know?"

"I want to know what an old-fashioned girl wears when she gets married?" I asked.

The water stopped. "Excuse me?"

"I think I just proposed."

"Marry you?" she asked.

"That's what I had in mind."

She turned the water back on and began to lather her hair. "I guess I'll wear jeans and boots."

"Thank you, ma'am."

The eggs were scrambled, fluffy and pretty good. The fake bacon was what it was, but I was getting used it. Not a thing one wants to say about food, I'm getting used to it, but better than the converse. I was on my second cup of tea and making eyes at Morgan.

"Well, if you two aren't absolutely disgusting, I just don't know what is." Gus said.

"Sorry, Gus," Morgan said.

I looked out the window to see that the snow was tapering off.

"What are you thinking about?" Morgan asked.

"I'm thinking that I have to go out in this mess and ride the fence. And I don't want to."

"Then don't," Gus said.

"I have to," I told him. "I need to check the line so I can take off some shoes and turn out a few horses."

"I'll keep the house warm for you," Gus said. "Yep, I'll just kick back, turn on one of them soap operas and keep it nice and toasty."

"Oh, yeah. And Gus, we're getting married," I said.

"To each other?" he asked.

"Do you two read the same joke book?"

Gus smiled at Morgan. "I think you're a damn fool, but I'm glad to hear it. Best wishes, little lady. And good luck."

"What about me?" I asked.

"You're one fortunate son of a bitch," he said. "So, when is this going to happen?"

Before Morgan could say we didn't know, the phone rang. I got up and answered it. It was Daniel White Buffalo.

"You must come out here again," Daniel said. He used "must" the way the Arapaho used it; it wasn't a command.

"What's going on?" I asked. "What's up this time? Another cow shot?" I laughed.

"Yes."

I stopped laughing. "Jesus, you're joking." But he wasn't joking. "Daniel, I don't know why you're calling me. I can't help."

"I think you should see this one," he said.

"I'm assuming this one looks a lot like the other one. Listen, Daniel, I'm behind as it is. I've got to ride my line."

"No, you must see this one." This was a command.

I studied the snow again through the window over the sink, considered the roads. I looked over at Morgan and shrugged. "Daniel, I'll be there in about an hour. I'll expect some hot tea when I get there." I hung up.

"What's that all about?" Gus asked.

"It appears that Daniel White Buffalo's got another dead beef. Wants me to look at it."

"What, are you the cow undertaker or something?" he asked.

"Must be."

"Would you like some company?" Morgan asked.

"No, you stay here. The roads are a mess," I said.

"What do you want me to do around here?" Gus asked.

"Keep the house warm," I said. "Morgan, would you lunge Felony and the App for me?"

"You bet."

I gave Morgan a kiss. "I'll see you two in a couple of hours."

"So, this is twice in a month," I said to Daniel White Buffalo as he approached. "People are going to start talking."

"Let 'em talk."

"Where's this one?"

"Not far from the other one." Daniel's usually cheerful face was wiped somewhat blank.

"It's too bad about the animal, Daniel. This is getting to be too much. Have you called Bucky yet?"

"What good is it to call him?" the man asked. He removed his cap and scratched his head. "He didn't do anything the last time and he won't do anything this time. I guess there's not much he can do."

"I suppose," I said. "Your rig or mine?"

"Mine," he said. "My truck knows the way."

We walked to his Bronco and I had to brush snow off the seat. "You ever cover this up?"

"When I remember." He started the engine.

"Why am I here, Daniel? I can't help any more than the sheriff. I can help less that the sheriff."

"You'll see."

We didn't say anything during the short, bouncy drive. I sat back, pulled my coat tight around me, dipping my face into my collar to keep warm, and enjoyed the view of the rolling landscape. Daniel stopped and set the brake a hundred or so yards upstream from where he'd shown me the first cow. This one was on the far bank as well, but today the creek was frozen. I skated, not intentionally, to the other side. This time Daniel followed.

The cow's head was a bloody mess; he'd been shot a few times. And this time the animal had been ripped through its middle and so the ground under it was soaked with blood. The blood had drained down the slope and melted snow to the water's edge. The ground was stained black.

"Well, I'd say this is pretty ugly," I said. "Tell me, when did it stop snowing here?"

"Last night, early this morning," Daniel said. "But this is not what I called you out here to see."

I looked at him.

"It's up here," he said. He turned and climbed the slope to flat ground, pointed down with a nod of his head.

I stood next to him and looked down at a bright blue tarp laid open over the snow. It looked like a thousand blue tarps. My mind raced and I imagined that there was a dead human under the cover.

Daniel bent over, grabbed a corner of the tarp, and pulled it away. Written in the snow, in red, in cow's blood, were the words *Red Nigger*.

I blew out a soft whistle of a breath. "I don't suppose you're the one who wrote that," I said.

"Pretty scary, eh?"

I nodded. "This makes my list of scary things."

"So, what do I do?" Daniel asked.

"I'm afraid I have no idea." I looked around at the ground around the writing, then started to pace a circle around it. I stopped and looked at some blue in the sky. "I say you call the sheriff."

"I'll consider that as an option, but what should I do?"

"Lock your doors, I guess. Face it, there are some bad folks in the neighborhood."

"And I'll keep a rifle loaded as well," he added.

I couldn't argue with that.

"You know, I have half a mind to camp out here and wait for the bastards," he said.

"And you might end up with half a mind," I said, looking at his eyes. "You can't sleep out here every night. Just to end up getting shot yourself." I began to circle the area again, looking for anything, maybe more shell casings. "I sure as hell wouldn't park myself out here."

"I should just let them kill my stock, kill my livelihood?"

"Listen, I'll come back and help you round them up," I said. "We can at least move them closer to the house."

Daniel just shook his head.

"Well, think about it. I'm glad to come back and help. All you have to do is call." I put a hand on his shoulder. "Come on, let's go."

We slid down the bank and made our way across the creek to the Bronco. "And call Bucky," I said.

"I'll call him," Daniel said.

The largest presence on Christmas morning was Emily's absence. The three of us didn't celebrate the day, but Gus insisted on cooking a big meal, big insofar as he would be preparing real meat, moose steaks from the freezer, a gift from the Gunthers in the fall. That morning, Morgan and I lay in the warm bed silently watching the sky just beginning to turn light.

"I miss her," she said.

"Me, too."

There wasn't much else to say. If Morgan were going to cry, she would cry. I'd hold her until she stopped crying. But she didn't cry.

"Mother always gave the horses carrots on Christmas," she said. "Can we do that this morning?"

"Of course."

We pulled on our clothes and went down to the kitchen. We found a bag of carrots in the refrigerator. I had a thought that Gus wanted the carrots for the dinner and when I looked at Morgan I knew she was thinking the same thing. I shrugged and closed the door.

"Are you sure?" Morgan whispered.

"I won't say anything if you don't," I said.

We went outside and began passing out carrots, one animal at a time. The mule was loose and following us, so he got several.

"What's the mule's name again?" Morgan asked, watching him walk away from us toward the hay once it was clear we were out of carrots. "His name is Pest now. He's mine. I don't like it, but I like him."

"That thing at Daniel's scares me," she said.

"Yeah, I know."

"Do you think we've got some crazed militia assholes around here?" she asked. She was studying my eyes.

"I know we do. There might be only one or two or there might be fifty, but they're out there. I'd be a fool to think there weren't."

Morgan pulled my arm to her and hugged me. "John, I don't want anything to happen to you."

"Nothing's going to happen to me. Nothing's going to happen to any of us. I'm very cautious and, besides, I've got old Gus."

"What will you do if they come around here?" she asked. "What are we supposed to do?"

That was a really good question and I didn't want to let on that I had absolutely no idea.

"I mean the sheriff is an hour away."

"Sweetie, things happen in a second. It doesn't matter whether Bucky is a minute away. This is my home."

"You sound like my mother."

"Thank you," I said. "I've lived here for twenty years. It's been good so far. No Son of Sam, no LAPD, and, until now, no neo-Nazis. Everything will be fine." I put my arm around her and pulled her close. "Let's go in and have some coffee and a little something to gnaw on."

Morgan and I sat at the table with our coffee and toast. Gus was at the refrigerator and he was pulling out things, surveying the stores. "I was sure I had a bag of carrots," he said. "Did you move my carrots?"

When neither of us spoke, he let the door swing shut. "I asked if anyone moved my carrots."

"Morgan, the man asked you a question," I said.

"John ate them," she said.

"I don't believe you," he said, flatly.

"We fed them to the horses," she said.

"That, I believe." He glared at us for a second. "How am I supposed to make glazed carrots without carrots?"

"We're sorry," I said.

"Well, you got that right."

"My mother always gave the horses carrots on Christmas."

Gus softened. "And a fine tradition it is."

The phone rang. Gus answered it. "He's right here," he said.

Morgan looked worried.

"I'm not going anywhere," I said. I took the phone from Gus. "Hello."

"Hi, John, it's me, David."

I was thrown. It took me a second to realize it was Howard's David. "David, how are you? Happy holiday."

"Merry Christmas," he said. He sounded subdued.

"So, how are things?"

"Okay," he said. "Well, not so hot."

"I'm sorry. Problems with your folks?"

"No, nothing like that. John, would you mind if I came out there and worked at your place next semester? I'm going to take some time off."

I was really caught off guard now. "Hold on for a second," I said. I slapped my hand over the mouthpiece. "It's David," I said to Gus and Morgan. "He wants to come here for the semester."

Gus made a face.

"Is he okay?" Morgan asked.

I put the phone back to my ear. "David, are you all right?"

"Robert and I broke up," he said.

"You broke up?" I repeated for the benefit of Morgan and Gus.

"He cheated on me. He slept with one of our friends."

"That's awful." I could hear his pain. "It's cold as hell out here, but you're welcome to come out. I do need to build a shed and put up some fencing."

"I'll work hard."

"I know you will, son," I said.

"I thought I'd fly into Denver and take the bus up to Highland the 28th. I don't have it all figured out."

"Of December?"

"Is that too early? It's just that I really want to get out of here

"No, that's fine. Just call and tell me when to meet you," I sai

He agreed to that and I hung up. "Is that okay?" I asked Morgan

"What happened?" she asked.

"That Robert-boyfriend-guy slept with someone else, one o friends. He sounded awful. Love trouble."

"Of course it's all right if he comes here," she said.

"He can't talk to his father?" Gus said.

"I think it's great that he thought he could call you," Morg "He needs to be able to talk to somebody."

"I suppose." I sat at the table, slouched, and stared up at th "I guess this is okay. Sure, it will be fine. I should give Howar though, let him know where his kid is going to be. That soun

"Yes," Morgan said.

The first thing Howard said when he was apprised of the si was, "Why did he call you and not me?"

"You two have had your problems," I said.

"But I'm his father."

"That's true and maybe that's what makes it so hard. I know. I just thought I'd let you know he's going to be her

"What exactly happened?"

"I don't know," I lied. "He said he needed to take som from school and said he wanted to work here on the ranc

"He didn't say why?"

I couldn't bring myself to lie again or didn't believe I would do it effectively, so I said, "He's arriving later this week."

"You think I've pushed him away by disapproving of his life-style?" he said.

I didn't lie this time. "That's probably true."

Howard was silent for a few seconds. "Thanks for calling to let me know. You're a good friend, John."

"Sure thing."

Dinner was wonderful, even without the glazed carrots. The moose steaks were sweet and tender, Gus's dressing was moist and peppery, and the sweet potatoes were covered with little melted marshmallows. Then there were the Brussels sprouts. Gus made up small plates of moose meat for Zoe and the puppy. The dogs finished their treat in a matter of seconds and looked up for more.

"If the horses can have their Christmas meal, then so can the dogs," he said. Then he sat down and lowered his head.

Morgan glanced to me. It looked like Gus was praying before his meal, but he never did that.

"Gus?" I asked.

He raised his head and looked at us.

"Are you all right?" Morgan asked.

"A little dizzy, queasy all of a sudden," he said.

"Have some water." I handed him his water glass.

"Maybe it's the wine I drank earlier," he said. "I shouldn't have had any, but I sneaked a sip."

"Still dizzy?"

"A little."

"That's it, we're going to the hospital," I said, pulling my napkin from my lap and putting it on the table.

"No, it's going away," he said.

I looked across the table at Morgan. She was terrified.

"Gus," I started.

But he cut me off. "I'm going to stretch out on the sofa. If I don't feel better in a few minutes, then you can take me in."

"Okay," I agreed.

I helped him up and he walked fairly steadily into the den and to the sofa. I stood there staring down at him, feeling useless.

"You go finish dinner," he said. "I didn't toil over that damn stove all day so no one would enjoy it."

"I'll come back in a few minutes."

In the kitchen, Morgan was pacing. I knew that she was reliving that last day with her mother. "We have to take him in," she said.

"Let's give him the couple of minutes he asked for," I said. I wasn't certain it was the wisest course, but I didn't want to upset him. "Just a couple minutes."

We sat down, but we didn't eat.

Gus came into the room. "I said for you two to eat." He walked, fairly steadily on his own, to the sink where he poured himself a glass of water. "I'm an old man. These spells happen. I feel better now."

"You're sure?" Morgan said.

Gus nodded. "You eat. I'm going to go upstairs and rest."

"Need help?" I asked.

"Eat!"

"Okay, but tomorrow, we're going to see the doctor," I said.

"All right."

All Gus told me after his visit to the doctor was that there had to be an adjustment in his blood-pressure medication and that he'd have to go down to Laramie for tests in a couple weeks. He'd also been prescribed a few other things, but as usual his dealings with his physician were kept close to him. While we waited at the pharmacy for the drugs, the sheriff walked in.

"Bucky," I said. I didn't rise from the green vinyl seat.

"Hey, John. Merry Christmas. How you doing, Gus?"

Gus nodded. The old man had always been cool when it came to the sheriff. I thought at times that it was simply the badge, at others that there was in fact something about Bucky that put him off.

"Did Daniel White Buffalo give you a call?" I asked.

"He did. And I drove out there and I saw it and I don't know what the hell to do. That's the skinny."

"What do you think?"

"What is there to think? I hope they're passing through. I hope lightning strikes them." He looked over at the sound of the bell on the door. "All I know is this is going to be my last term."

"Daniel's pretty upset," I said.

"I don't blame him," Bucky said. "What about you?"

"What about me?"

"Are you upset?"

"Yeah, I'm upset," I said. "Don't you think I should be upset?"

"Yeah, I think so."

The pharmacist came over, and Gus got up to talk to him.

"How's Morgan?" Bucky asked.

"She's okay," I said. "She's at her place trying to close it up. We moved her animals to my place a couple weeks ago. I have to tell you, this stuff scares her."

Bucky nodded. "I'll have Hanks swing by your place periodically. I've got someone doing the same thing at White Buffalo's."

"That's good," I said.

As we walked back to the truck, I asked Gus why he didn't like Bucky.

"He gives me the willies," he said. "Can't say why. It's in my gut. I don't like him."

"Fair enough."

Once in the truck and rolling out of town, I asked, "Won't you tell me what the doctor told you?"

"Same stuff."

"That might mean something to me if I heard the first stuff," I said. "What kind of tests are you going to have?"

"The usual crap. A tube here, a tube there. He wants to check out my colon again. He seems to like that."

"But they did that at the hospital here last time," I said.

"I think it's a scheduling thing, I don't know."

I didn't press. Gus was going to the doctor, taking care of things. My knowing wasn't going to change what he would or wouldn't do. It was his business and I would let him see to it.

"Well, if you want to talk about it, I'm here," I said.

"I know, John."

NINE

THE BIG SILVER GREYHOUND from Laramie was on time in spite of the foul weather, mainly because the trip did not involve the interstate freeway. When the highway was being planned in the sixties, the ranchers told the highway folks that the chosen route was a bad one. The ranchers suggested the old road. The completed freeway came to be called the Snow Chi Minh Trail and was closed quite a bit during the winter. The old road became the alternate and always-open route. Twenty minutes after greeting David, I was saying good-bye to Gus as he boarded another bus for Casper. The old man would arrive that evening, check into the Motel 6 next door to the hospital, not eat or drink anything after six, and be ready for his exams the next morning. Gus had refused my driving him, saying one, "I ain't no baby and I can take care of myself," and two, "Besides, you've got a guest coming into town." So, David and I waved good-bye to the bus. Gus didn't really notice and seemed older to me.

David and I wandered down the street toward the restaurant where we had first met. The snow was dirty and a bit more charming because of it. We walked in and were seated at the same table by the same young woman, who took the same interest in David.

""You came back for the good weather, I see," she said.

"I guess so," David said.

"How are you, today?" I asked her.

"I'm fine. As long as I'm inside, I'm fine. What would you two gentlemen like to drink?"

"Coffee," David said.

"Tea for me," I said. "Earl Grey and some milk with that?"

"Coming up," she said and walked away.

"How are you, my friend?" I asked.

David shrugged.

"Relationships," I sighed. "They're always difficult. Things don't always go the way we plan. Blah, blah, blah, and all the other inane platitudes that you've already heard fifty times."

David laughed.

"What I meant to say was, doesn't life suck?"

He laughed again, fell quiet for a few seconds. Then, "I really trusted Robert. I think I'm one of the those people who's too quick to fall in love."

I nodded. "Could be. Personally, I thought Robert was an asshole."

"Really?"

"Big-time," I said. "And I'm not just saying that because it's true."

"He was a little older, sure of himself, cute. I just missed all the signals." He looked out the window.

"Signals?" I asked.

"They seem obvious now. Going out and not telling me where he was, late-night phone calls, the phone would ring and if I answered no one was there. His own narcissism should have tipped me off."

"Hindsight," I said.

"I should never have moved in with him," David said.

"It's never a good idea to rush things," I said.

The waitress delivered our coffee and tea, smiled admiringly at David, took our food orders, and left again.

"Have you talked to your parents?"

"I called my mother and we sort of talked, you know what I mean. What's there to say?"

"Listen, I need to tell you that I let your father know you were going to be here," I said. "I hope you don't mind."

"I guess not."

"I should have talked to you first. I'm sorry."

"No," David said, "really, it's all right. What's it matter anyway? It's no secret."

I poured some milk in my tea. "I don't mean to sound stupid," I said. "I just kind of do that naturally, but I wanted to ask you something."

"Yes?"

"When did you realize you were gay?"

"That's not stupid," David said, generously.

"My experience is limited and I'm just curious."

"When I was ten I knew I was different and when I was thirteen I knew I was gay." David sipped his coffee. "I don't know how, but I knew it. I kept it to myself until I was out of the house because of the way I'd hear my father talk about fags and queers. He scared me."

"I can imagine. I didn't mean to bring up bad memories," I said.

"I know. So, what's new with you?"

"I'm getting married."

David didn't say anything, but he set his mug down.

"You remember Morgan? Well, she's the victim. She's living at the ranch now."

"That's great," he said, though I doubted he meant it.

"Kind of living there. We have her ranch as well. We're going to put it on the market."

"What does Morgan do?" David asked.

"She has taught some courses at the community college, literature and composition, but not for a while. For several years she was mostly caring for her mother who just died."

"That's great. About your getting married, I mean."

We stopped by Morgan's ranch on the way home. She had built a fire, and smoke was coming from the chimney; the place looked postcard pretty in the late afternoon.

"We've moved her horses to my place," I said as I killed the engine. "This is a sweet place. It's going to be hard for her to let it go."

Morgan met us at the door. Zoe was standing behind her and behind Zoe was the coyote, well formed, still with three legs and fuzzy. She was redder than I thought she would be.

"Morgan, you remember David," I said.

"Of course I do," she said. She gave David a hug, then kissed me.

"The puppy's really gotten bigger," David said. He kneeled down and stroked both dogs. The coyote was not nippy, I liked that, and appreciated the attention.

"Gus get off okay?" Morgan asked.

"Yep."

"What's the puppy's name?" David asked.

"Gus named him after my mother," Morgan said. "Her name is Emily."

"She's really strong," David said.

"So, how's it going here?" I asked.

"Getting there," she said. "Mother had a lot of papers."

"We all do," I said.

"What do you say we kill the fire and head home?" Zoe came and pushed her nose under my hand. "Have I been ignoring you, girl?" I said to the dog. "I'm sorry." I rubbed behind her ear. "We'll all ride together. We'll come back for your truck tomorrow."

"I just want to grab a few things," Morgan said. Then to David, "How was your trip? Was the bus cold?"

"If anything it was too hot," David said. "The flight into Denver was bumpy. I'm not a fan of flying."

"Who is?" Morgan asked.

"Get your stuff," I said. "I'll kill the fire. David, would you walk outside with the dogs and make sure the pup stays close?"

"Sure." David left with the dogs.

"How's he doing?" Morgan asked.

"Fine, I guess." I put my arms around Morgan. "I missed you."

"See, I knew you were a big pussycat. You're not going to change after we get married, are you?"

"Well, I hope being around you will make me better looking," I said.

"Keep wishing, cowboy."

Back at my place, I prepared dinner while Morgan and David went out to muck stalls. The temperature was plummeting and I asked them to throw blankets over a couple of the older animals. Morgan came in complaining about my being in the warm house and I told her that cooking was man's work. David closed the door, took off his jacket, and slapped his arms.

"This is worse than Chicago," he said.

"Chicago can be pretty cold," I said. "David, I decided to let you have the bedroom downstairs. It's down the hall off the den. I'm afraid the room upstairs is full of somebody's stuff."

"My stuff," Morgan said.

"The bathroom is close and you won't have to share it with Gus."

"Thanks. I think I'll check out the bathroom right now." David left the room.

"He's very quiet," Morgan said. "He hardly said two words while we were out there."

"Really? I guess he's shy." I said. "You know you can be pretty intimidating sometimes."

Morgan snuggled up close to me. "Oh, yeah? You think so, do you?"

"Yes, indeed. Downright overbearing."

She kissed me. "Little ol' me?"

"Yep. Now get out of here and let me cook. You make me nervous."

David returned. "The room looks great."

"It can be a little chilly in the morning. The wall heater in that bathroom is pretty good, though."

"Can I help?" he asked.

"You can help by sitting down and having a cup of tea while I do this," I said. "You, too, madam."

"I'm going upstairs to do a few things," Morgan said. "Fifteen minutes?"

"That's about right."

When Morgan was gone, David said, "She's nice."

"Yeah, she's something special."

"So, when is the wedding?"

"The spring, I guess." I poured olive oil and balsamic vinegar over the salad and gave it a toss.

"I never imagined ranch people eating like you," he said.

"All city people eat the same?" I asked.

"Okay, okay." David stood and walked to the window. "Does the mule always just wander around like that?"

"I can't stop him. Unfortunately, he's mine now. I call him Pest. He answers to it, so I guess it's his name."

"John, I want to thank you for letting me come here."

"You're welcome. I don't know if you're going to be thanking me tomorrow when we're riding the fence in ten-degree weather."

"You should probably know, I've never ridden a horse," David said.

I turned and looked at him. "Never? Not even a pony ride?"

The young man shook his head.

"Well, it will be a ten-degree riding lesson and then a fifteen-degree fence check. I'll put you on my old App; she's as safe as it gets."

"Have you ever fallen off a horse?"

"I've been bucked off and launched off, but I've never fallen off a horse. You ever fall off a chair?"

"Chairs don't move," he said.

"Well, if you can sit on a chair without falling off, you can sit on a horse. You'll like it." I heard Morgan coming down the stairs. "David, why don't you grab some plates out of that cupboard behind you."

"It's not ready?" Morgan said.

I gave the salad another toss. "Shadup and sidown," I said. "But first, grab some silverware."

She opened the drawer. "Don't listen to him, David," she said. "This is not silver. I'm not sure what it is."

David chuckled.

"He's not a bad cook, though," Morgan said. "He's kind of a keeper."

The next morning was clear and hard cold. David was bundled up in a down coat and wore a watch cap pulled down over his ears. We finished the feeding, ate some cereal, and saddled the App for his lesson.

In the round pen I told him the basics of reining. "Touch her neck on the left side with the rein and she'll go right. You don't have to pull. The horse will go where your belly button points. Point your navel to where you want to go, lay the rein on her neck and you're off. Now, give her a little kiss sound and a squeeze with your calves."

He did and the horse walked.

"Go ahead and walk her around the circle."

David was awkward, but the horse was confident and soon he looked comfortable enough.

"That's all we're going to do is walk," I said.

"What if something scares her?" he asked.

"This old girl is bomb proof. But if a spaceship does land and gets her running, hang on and realize that she's the least of your worries."

We rode out the gate and toward the southeast.

"What are we doing again?"

"Duncan Camp wants to park some cattle on BLM adjacent to my place and I want to make sure my fence is good."

"A range war," David joked.

"That's right. No, not really, but I don't want his cows coming close and messing up things. I don't much like cows, if you haven't noticed. Besides, it will be easier for him to find the beasts if they can't wander across my place and find their way onto the desert."

We rode the fence and re-stretched barbed wire in places, rolled up discarded wire and made sure the gates were in good shape and closed. The work and the sun warmed us up and soon we were a little sweaty in our coats.

"I'm getting hot," David said.

"Well, stay hot. Better to be hot in your coat. You take that jacket off and that cold hits your wet body and you'll be sorry."

"Got it."

We stopped on a ridge and looked down at the valley. "This is something, isn't it?" I said.

"It's beautiful."

"I never get used to it." I looked at him. "I'm glad you're here, David."

"Me, too. Thanks."

We came on one last sagging string of wire. David managed to tangle it around his leg. It ripped through his jeans and sliced his calf. He let out a scream and started hopping around.

"Let me see it," I said. "You're going to have to drop your pants."

"Jesus, that hurts." He undid his belt and exposed his leg.

I pulled my first aid kid from my saddlebag and began to treat the wound. "This is going to sting a little," I told him, then put some antiseptic on.

"A little?"

"Okay, a lot." I looked at the flap of skin. There wasn't a lot of blood. "You're not going to bleed to death. Tell me this, cowpoke, do you remember the last time you had a tetanus shot?"

"No."

"In the past ten years?"

"I don't know. I don't think so."

"Past five years?" I asked.

"No. I'm sure of that. Is that bad?"

I stared at the wound. "It would be real bad if we were in the middle of nowhere," I said.

David looked around and started to laugh. "I guess everything's relative. What now?"

"We drive into town and get you poked with a big needle," I said. "That way you won't get lockjaw and whooping cough and die before your time, leaving me to explain things to your parents."

"Don't sugarcoat it."

"A big, fat needle."

"That's better."

"Besides, you deserve a better dressing than the one I can give you," I said. "Mount up."

We dropped Morgan at her place and she planned to drive back in her car. We didn't have any wait at the hospital. David got his shot and we left. I decided I wanted to buy some flowers for Morgan, so we stopped in at the only florist shop in town. As we walked out to the Jeep, I saw the BMW parked across the street. The rednecks were just getting out as we were getting in. They shot me a look as we drove away. I don't think David saw them.

That night Gus called and told me what time his bus would be arriving the next day. He sounded low and I asked him how the tests went and he said he didn't know, only that they were uncomfortable and he was tired.

"How is he?" Morgan asked. She was sitting on the sofa in the study, reading.

"Tired."

"Thanks again for the flowers," she said.

"Pretty gal like you needs pretty things around her," I said in my best cowboy voice.

"You're the one who's tired," she said. "I'll pick up Gus tomorrow. You catch up around here. That will make three days into town in a row."

I couldn't argue with that. "Thanks, honey."

I fell onto the sofa next to her. "You know, I never called anybody else sweetie and honey before."

"Really?"

"Really."

"Where's our guest?"

"I think the young man has retired for the evening," I said. "It was a rough day for him. He was nervous the whole time he was on horseback."

"At least he's a sport," Morgan said.

"He's a good kid."

"He's not a kid. He's twenty years old."

"He's not a kid to you because you're a spring chicken," I said. "He's a kid to me because I'm old as dirt."

The phone rang and I walked across the room to the desk to answer it. It was Daniel White Buffalo.

"Another cow dead?" I asked.

"No, but Clara Monday thinks somebody took a shot at her," he said.

"Say again?"

"She was over in the Owl Creeks, just riding along, and she says somebody put a bullet into the slope behind her."

"Did she see anyone?" I asked.

"I don't think so." Daniel took a breath and listened to my silence. "I just thought you should know."

"Thanks, Daniel." I hung up.

"What is it?" Morgan asked, closing her book and leaning forward, seeing the expression on my face.

"It seems somebody fired a shot at Clara Monday."

"Oh, my god," she said.

"Daniel said he thought I should know."

Morgan walked over and put her arms around me.

"Don't worry," I said. I knew, however, that she could feel my uneasiness. I stroked her hair.

In my dream, I was dragging a reluctant donkey around a large pen. I was afraid she was going to colic and I didn't want her to roll. The vet had called and told me he would be right there, but that was hours ago. It was a hot day, sweltering, and I was drenched. The donkey would willingly walk a few steps with me then fall back on her heels, leaving me to drag her and her quarter-ton pendulous belly forward.

Then she would stop and try to cough up something and I began to think it was choke and not colic. Susie came out to the corral and told me that the vet had called and that he was on his way and that he was all worried that the donkey was going to die and so she was all worried that the donkey was going to die and I said, "Well, she isn't dying yet, so let's wait and worry when we know enough to worry about." This made her mad and she walked away into the house. I wanted to go after her, to tell her that my saying that was probably just a clumsy way of my expressing worry, but I couldn't leave the donkey. Every time I tried to walk away from the donkey, she moved as if to lie on her side, so I would start tugging again. The vet showed up and Susie joined him as he walked toward the donkey and me. Just as they reached the gate, the donkey hacked up a black piece of plastic. The vet sighed relief and said, "So, it was choke." He turned to Susie and said, "I'm sorry I got you all worked up."

I said to the vet, "We were both pretty nervous, all right."

"Well, I'll take a look," the vet said. "We'll put a tube down her and pump in some oil to be sure everything's going where it ought to be going."

Susie had turned away and was marching to the house.

I followed her inside, but couldn't find her anywhere. I looked in all the rooms and then in the barn. The vet was riding the donkey around in the pen. I looked out across the field and saw footprints in the snow, even though it was hot, but I didn't follow them. I just went back into the house and tried to start a fire, but every match I lit went out and I became more and more frustrated. Finally, my hands were trembling and the matches wouldn't even spark.

"John." Morgan woke me. Her voice broke through and when I opened my eyes I saw the hint of sunrise through the window.

"Yes?"

"You were having a bad dream." She used her thumb to stroke the furrow of my brow.

I put my arm around her and pulled her close. Her skin was bare and warm. "Was I kicking and screaming like a dang fool?"

"No, just muttering."

"Sorry about that," I said. "What time is it?"

"Five-forty-five. We're burning daylight."

"I might as well get up then."

She pushed me back down. "Oh, yeah?"

"Why, do you have something else in mind?"

"Maybe," she said.

"I get it," I said. "You want us to sleep for another half-hour. I can do that." And I turned over.

Morgan poked me in the side and made me jump. "You'd better show me some cowboy lovin' or you're in for it."

"Oh, all right, if I have to."

I fed the horses and groomed those whose turn it was. Then I worked Felony in the round pen for a while. He had really come along and it was about time to let him go home to Duncan Camp. He'd begun a fairly steady ride and his big body let him cover ground in a hurry, even if it did make him a little clumsy on steep terrain. I cantered around a few more times, then stopped in the center of the ring and looked up at the sky. The sun was out and the only clouds were well away over the mountains. The day promised to be mild, but those clouds were going to make things bad, I just knew it in my gut. I'd asked Morgan if she wanted to saddle Square and take a ride into the high country with me, but she said she was going to make bread. She suggested I take David up there. He and Gus were sleeping late. I figured that they deserved it on New Year's Eve. I left Felony saddled and tied at the post outside the kitchen.

Morgan was measuring flour into a bowl next to the sink. David was at the table, dressed and finishing a bowl of cereal.

"How about a ride in the hills?" I asked. I could see that he was apprehensive. "Nothing fancy. You'll be used to this in no time. It's not necessary to ride a horse to work on a ranch, but it's the fun part. Unless that leg's going to give you trouble."

"No, it'll be all right."

"We don't have to go out," I said.

"No, really, I want to," he said. "I'll just run and brush my teeth." He left the room.

"I didn't push him, did I?" I looked to Morgan.

She shook her head. "No. But it's kind of cute."

"What is?"

"That kid really wants to please you." She cracked an egg into the bowl. "He looks up to you."

"He doesn't even know me," I said.

"Well, that would explain it," Morgan said.

"Very funny." I poured myself half a cup of coffee. "You feed the puppy yet?"

"Yep. She's really growing. She's got a nice temperament."

"And what are you making?"

"Cookies," she said. "I woke up and felt like making cookies. I'm praying that David loves cookies because I don't want to eat them all myself."

"Is Gus still in bed?"

Morgan nodded.

I looked at the clock. It was almost eight-thirty. "I think I'll check on him. You think I should?"

"Please," Morgan said.

I walked up the stairs and tapped on Gus's door. "Hey, Gus."

"Yeah?" he answered.

I felt a load lift from me. "You okay in there?"

"I'm fine," he said, gruffly. "That bus ride took it out of me. I'll be down in a while."

"You bet. No rush."

I walked back down the stairs and into the kitchen. David was in the mud room, pulling on his boots.

"How is he?" Morgan asked.

"I think he's just tired. He said he'll be down soon."

"Maybe I should take him up some juice," she said.

I shook my head. "I don't think that's a good idea."

Morgan understood and went back to the counter. "See you later, sweetie," I said giving her a kiss on the cheek. "Sure you won't come?"

"Have a good ride."

"Ready to ride, cowboy?" I stepped out of my house shoes and into my own boots. "Let's go pop some brush."

David, like many people on their second time in the saddle, was tense and trying to feel in control, so he held the reins short in a tight fist and clamped his legs around the horse.

"Let her have her head," I said. "Give her some slack. Relax your body. Let it go." I took a deep breath and let it out to show him.

He eased up.

"Take another breath," I said. "Let it all out."

He did.

"Now, you relax and let the horse do the walking."

We rode out through the south gate and toward the hills.

"How'd you sleep?" I asked.

"Pretty well. That room is nice and warm."

"It's the warmest room in the house and I have no idea why. It's a little tight in there, I know."

We rode on a ways and David began to relax a little with the App. She was a good horse, but she was still a thousand pounds of non-thinking muscle and I didn't want David to forget that.

We started up a slope, my horse following his. "Take your down-hill foot out of the stirrup on the steep. That way, if something goes bad you'll fall to the closest ground and not under the horse."

That made David tense up again.

"I told you that because it's true and because you should never forget you're on a horse when you are, in fact, on a horse."

"Have you ever been hurt on a horse?" David asked.

"Sure." I looked down the hillside at the frozen creek. I thought about Susie and didn't say anything else.

"John?"

"Yeah?"

"Something wrong?"

"No, not at all. How are you doing up there?"

"Good. I feel pretty good." He looked up the slope. "What kind of animals do you have around here?"

"Elk, antelope, deer, the occasional mountain sheep. We have bears, black and grizzly. They're all sleeping right now. And of course we have coyotes and a wolf now and again."

"Everything is so beautiful," he said.

"Take the trail to the left," I told him. "I want to show you something."

We followed the trail to a ridge that overlooked a lower hill and beyond that was the Red Desert, red in the midday light, just like its name implied, stretching out forever, a butte standing sentinel in the middle of it.

"My god," David said.

"This is why I live here," I said. "Every time I come up here and look at that I know my place in the world. It's okay to love something bigger than yourself without fearing it. Anything worth loving is bigger than we are anyway."

"That sounds almost religious," David said.

"I wouldn't know anything about religion," I said. "I know this is my life and this is my place."

"My mother is a Catholic," David said.

I nodded.

"She's full of guilt. I don't think her religion makes her happy."

"Well, that's no good," I said. "Come on, let's head back. I'm starting to feel the cold."

Gus was up and playing with the coyote, who had taken to the game of fetch. Gus would slide a balled-up sock across the kitchen linoleum and the puppy would scamper after it, grab it, and then demonstrate her instinct by shaking the thing until dead. Only then would she drag the by-now-unrolled sock back to Gus.

"What a gorgeous day," I said, looking out the window.

Gus balled up the sock and threw it again. "Do you want green beans or spinach with dinner?" he asked.

"Whatever you want," I said. "Where's Morgan?"

"She's in the study going over her mother's papers." Gus groaned as he pushed himself up from a knee and into a chair. "Speaking of which, I've got some papers I want to go over with you."

"Okay," I said.

"How's the boy?" Gus asked.

"He's good. I've got him out there grooming a couple of animals."

The phone rang and I picked up. It was Howard.

"Almost Happy New Year," I said.

"So, how do I get to your place from Highland?" he asked.

"Excuse me?"

"Surprise. I'm in Highland. I rented a car in Denver and here I am. How do I get there?"

I gave him directions. "See you in a while," I said. As I hung up David came into the house, sat on the bench in the mud room, and began to remove his boots.

"What is it?" he asked, noticing what must have been puzzlement on my face. "What's going on?"

"It seems your father is on his way here."

"What are you talking about?"

"He just called. He flew to Denver, rented a car, and now he's in Highland. He'll be here in about an hour."

"Fuck," David said.

I nodded.

"Fuck," he repeated and walked away in his stocking feet toward his room in the back.

Morgan came in. "What was that all about?"

Gus said, "We're having company. The boy's father is on his way." He turned to me. "Put on some tea water."

TEN

THE DAY HAD GONE SOUR in more ways than one. The sky had turned slate gray and was beginning to spawn fat snowflakes. Weather Wally had actually predicted heavy snow and the face of the day had caused me to summarily dismiss him. I was standing out in front of the house in the near dark watching the storm get bad. It had been two hours since Howard's call and I was growing concerned. Zoe and the pup were out sniffing and taking care of matters.

David came out and joined me. "It's so cold."

"This is blowing in out of the north. I sure didn't see it coming. Maybe you should go back inside."

"No, I'm okay. Hey, I wanted to thank you for the ride today. That was great, beautiful."

"You're welcome."

"You looked good on horseback. How'd it feel?"

"Better. Not bad, really." He jumped a little to keep warm. "I liked it. Jesus, I've never been this cold." He looked at the snow in the sky above us. "John, have you ever been hurt on a horse?"

"Sure. But hell, you can get hurt getting out of the bathtub, but you're not going to stop taking baths." I looked at the boy's face. "My wife was killed by a horse. Actually, she caused it. She tried to get on a horse that wasn't ready when she wasn't ready and things got bad in a hurry."

"Jesus."

"Six years ago. I miss her." I spotted headlights on the ridge. "There he is," I said. "You're sure you're all right?"

"I'll be okay. I'm a little nervous."

I nodded.

He pulled his jacket tighter around his body.

"It's going to get colder, too," I told him.

The car bounced along the drive toward us and stopped. Howard got out and so did a woman.

"Who's that?" David asked me, softly.

"I don't know," I whispered. The woman was wrapped in a long down coat and her blond hair squirted from the edges of her fuzzy cap. I walked toward Howard. David hung back.

"John!" Howard greeted me with a hug. "John, I'd like you to meet Pamela. Pamela this is the famous John Hunt."

"Hey, John," Pamela said. She was young, young enough that I took time to think that she was young.

Howard had the back door open and was pulling out a couple of bags. "The drive over here was a mess. The snow is getting bad."

"Let me take one of those," I said.

"No, I wouldn't hear of it," Howard said. He turned and looked toward David and the house.

"And is that my son?"

"Hi, Dad."

I wrested one of the bags away from Howard anyway. He walked with Pamela toward the house. I followed.

"Pamela, this is my son, David."

"David, this is Pamela."

David nodded a greeting. Howard tried awkwardly to hug his son while he held a bag slung over his shoulder.

"Let's get inside where it's warm," I said. David led the way and I brought up the rear. I cast a glance at the snowy night, before entering. Howard made all the introductions. Pamela was even younger in full light. If she was older than David, it was only by months.

"What a sweet house," Pamela said. She unbuttoned her big lavender coat and peeled out of it. She needed the coat. The blouse she wore worked hard to contain her breasts and her low-slung jeans revealed occasional flashes of her navel. Her boots were oddly appropriate for the weather.

Morgan showed absolutely no reaction, good horsewoman that she was, but Gus turned away and walked into the kitchen. He said over his shoulder that he would put on some coffee and water for tea.

"I'm very pleased to meet you, Morgan," Howard said.

"Me, too." Morgan looked at the luggage. "You'll be sleeping in the study. It's a sofa bed and we hope it doesn't kill you."

"We'll be fine," Howard said. "Won't we, Pamela?"

"Of course," Pamela said.

David stood at a distance and watched, his face fairly blank. His eyes were angry, his body showed fear, his fingers tapping against his thigh, his Adam's apple moving with his swallowing.

"I'll help Gus while Morgan shows you the study," I said. I walked into the kitchen and closed the door.

"That young lady needs to put on some clothes," Gus said. Gus shook his head. "What is that man thinking? Why'd he bring her here?"

"I don't know, Gus."

"Why is he here at all?"

I shrugged.

David came into the room.

"How are you?" I asked.

David barked out a laugh.

"That's what I say," Gus said.

Morgan came into the kitchen, looked behind herself as she closed the door. "What is wrong with that man?" she asked. "They're freshening up."

"I hope that means getting dressed," Gus said.

"Thank you," Morgan said.

"I'm sorry, David," I said.

Why is he here?" David walked to the window and looked out at the snow. "Hell, he can't even leave now."

"Got that right," Gus said. He sat at the table and whistled for the coyote. Emily came and sat to have her head stroked.

"Well, they're here," I said. "Let's make the best of it. Gus, do we have enough food?"

"Plenty of food," Gus said.

"They're coming," Morgan said and stepped away from the door toward me.

"That room will be just fine," Howard said.

"It's sweet," Pamela said. "It has a real, ranchy, rustic feel. And I like all the wood." Then she spotted the puppy under Gus's hand. "Oh, look at the puppy. What kind of puppy?" She made kissing sounds to call the dog, but as long as Gus was touching her, she was not moving.

Gus stopped petting Emily. "She's a coyote," he said. "Her mother was killed and she lost her leg."

"Oh, poor thing." Pamela squatted and I was fearful her breast would pop free. She kissed again and this time the puppy hopped over to her. "Poor thing," she said again.

Zoe watched from the corner, stretched out on her bed. She was attending mainly to David, I assumed because he appeared upset.

The coyote wandered away in midstroke and sat again beside Gus.

"You're welcome to build a fire in the little stove," I said. "The big stove in the other room keeps things pretty warm, but that one's nice when lit."

"Thank you," Pamela said.

Howard walked over and put his arm over David's shoulder. "It's good to see you, son. I came so I could have a little time with you."

David looked at his father and then at Pamela. "I promised Gus I'd help get the meal ready right now."

"Of course," Howard said. Then he looked at me. "Oh yeah. Pammy, would you run to the room and get that gift?"

Pamela left the kitchen.

"I brought you a little something," Howard said. "This is a really nice place. I'm looking forward to seeing it in the light."

"I talked to Mom," David said.

"And how is she?" Howard asked.

"She sounds really strong now," David said. "Like she's found herself somehow."

"That's great," Howard said. "That's what I always wanted for her."

Pamela came back into the room and handed me a wrapped bottle. I thanked her and stared at the blue ribbon.

"Open it," Howard said. "It's a bottle of Scotch. I thought I remembered that you like Scotch."

"Thank you." I peeled down the paper and looked at the label. "Glenturret," I read. "I've never heard of that."

"It's a nineteen-eighty," Pamela said. "It's aged in special cherry-wood barrels. It's got a nice flavor."

"Thank you. What a nice gift."

"Pamela knows all about whiskys and wines," Howard said.

"I'll bet," David said.

"Is that your business?" Morgan asked.

"No, just a hobby," Pamela said.

"What is your business?" David asked.

"Our flight into Denver was as smooth as silk," Howard said. "That's some airport. We had a little trouble with the rental car. You see they stuck us in that midsize. I reserved an SUV, but they screwed it up. It would have been good on a night like tonight."

"No kidding," David said.

"Why don't we go into the other room and let Gus get on with the meal," Morgan said.

"That's a good idea," Gus said. Then, to David, "And you stay in here and help me, youngblood."

Morgan followed Pamela and Howard out of the kitchen. I started after them and stopped at the door. "Are you okay, David?"

David nodded.

The guests, Morgan and I sat in the living room. The stove doors were open and the fire actually looked beautiful.

"It's like a postcard," Pamela said.

"Let's break open that Scotch," Howard said.

"I'll get it," Morgan said. She touched my leg as she got up.

"So, it was a messy drive," I said.

"Just awful," Howard said. "I could hardly see the road." He looked at Pamela beside him. "But Pamela helped. Right, Pammy? We got gas in that funny little station at the edge of town. I went in to pay first and he told me to go ahead and pump it and then come back and pay."

"So trusting," Pamela said.

"You don't do that in New York, I can tell you that." Howard smiled at Morgan's reappearance with the whisky. "There we are."

Morgan put the tray with the bottle and glasses on the coffee table. "I thought I'd let you pour your own. I'm having water."

"If you don't mind," I said, "I'll have water as well."

"It is early," Howard said. "But it was a long drive." He leaned forward and poured a little into two glasses.

Morgan poured half her water into my glass.

"To the new year," Howard said.

We touched glasses and drank.

"That's exquisite," Howard said. "You'll have to try this later."

I nodded. "So, how is the law business?"

"Boring. Basically, I don't like my clients. Every one of them thinks that he is my only client. They call me at home and expect me to remember the details of their particular cases."

"Howard is a tax attorney," I told Morgan. "In college, he wanted to be a civil rights lawyer."

"So, what happened?" Pamela asked Howard.

"Marriage and kid," Howard said, flatly. He leaned forward and poured himself a little more Scotch. "When you're young, it's easy to be idealistic. It doesn't cost anything. Now, John here, he's managed to stay idealistic. He said he wanted to live on a ranch with horses and that's what he's done. But John isn't like the rest of us. He built this place all by himself."

"I had plenty of help," I said.

"That's a John thing to say." Howard laughed. "This man is amazing. He's always been better than me at everything. Well, part of it was that he claimed to not want as much, but I don't know if that was true. What do you think, John?"

I shrugged. I didn't know what to make of his words or even the situation for that matter, perhaps especially the situation. I looked at Morgan and I could tell that if she knew of something to help me out, she would have been doing it. I had a mind to excuse myself to the kitchen for some reason or another, but I couldn't bring myself to leave Morgan alone with them.

"What do you do?" Morgan asked Pamela.

"I'm a paralegal," Pamela said. She said it without conviction, as if in some way it was not true.

"Pammy used to work in my firm, but no longer."

"I hope there was no problem," Morgan said.

"Only that we're getting married," Howard said. "My firm has a policy against fraternization."

"Congratulations, Howard," I said. "I don't suppose David knows anything about this yet?"

Howard shook his head.

We sat quietly for a while. Pamela reached over and held Howard's hand. I studied the man. He had been a friend for a long time and in all that time I was always confused about why he was my friend. We had little in common, aesthetically, socially or politically, and we'd never run in the same circles. Still, I had been the best man at his wedding and I was called the godfather of his son, though there was never any official church business. Susie had always flat-out hated him. Right at that second I was finding him somewhat objectionable and it made me feel bad about myself.

"We're getting married, too," Morgan said.

I smiled at her. It was the perfect thing to say. It eased the tension in the room and served to bring me back to the positive stuff in my life.

"Yes," I said. "Somehow I managed to trick her into it."

Gus stuck his head into the room and announced dinner, stating that it would be served in the main dining room.

"He's referring to the kitchen," I said.

At the table we sat in a painful stew of silence. The elk stew and the potato pancakes and the asparagus might have been as delicious as it all looked, but I could not taste any of it. I was worried about David and about what Howard might say and about what Howard would say and about what Gus might say as he watched Pamela lean her breasts over the table as she reached for the bread.

"Mother's fine," David said, for no apparent reason. Except that the reason was all too apparent.

"I'm glad to hear that, son," Howard said. Then, "Gus, this meal is fantastic. What kind of meat is in this stew?"

"Elk."

"You hear that, Pammy? Elk. We're on the frontier."

We were having wine with dinner and David was on his third glass. I didn't know how to slow him down. Then Gus caught his eye and said, "Go easy on the wine, son."

"David," Howard said. "I need to tell you something."

"What? That you're going to marry Pammy here?" David laughed, but the silence that followed his comment made him silent, too. "You're not serious."

"I'm very serious," Howard said. "Pamela and I have thought about it and we've decided it's the right thing to do."

"What do you know about the right thing to do?" David said.

"Son," Howard said.

"Don't *son* me." David shot me a glance, as if for help. "You haven't asked me once how I'm doing. I mean, really asked me. Well, I'll tell you. I broke up with Robert and I'm in a lot of pain."

"Robert," Howard said with disdain. "There will be other Roberts and there will be more pain. I don't understand the *Robert* thing."

"Of course you don't," David said. "You don't want to understand. You won't try to understand."

"Have you ever been with a girl?" Howard asked.

I scooted back from the table, my chair making the sound I wanted. "David, we'd better go check on the animals. It's going to be a rough night out there."

David studied my eyes for a second. I could feel the breath he let out. "I'll grab my jacket," he said.

The frigid wind was blasting through the barn. I pushed the north door closed after us. With the wind-tunnel effect gone, we were immediately more comfortable and we could hear each other.

"Let's check everybody's water and blankets," I said.

"Can you believe what you just heard?" David asked.

"I'm sorry, David."

"That woman is younger than I am," he said. "Roberts." David shook his head and then let out a scream.

I turned to a rustling sound and found the mule standing in an open stall. I chuckled.

"What is it?" David asked.

"This mule may be a lot of things, but he's not stupid. Throw him some hay and close him in." I looked down the barn line. "Then we'll walk the outside and make sure the outer stall doors are shut tight."

"What should I do?" David asked.

"I don't know," I said. "I suppose you can decide that though he's your father, he doesn't have to be your friend. You don't need his approval. You might want it; that's another thing. But you don't need it."

"That makes sense."

"And it was easy to say. Don't use me as any source of wisdom, David. Just remember: There is a large bird called a pelican, whose mouth can hold more than his belly can; he can hold in his beak enough food for a week and I don't how the hell he can."

"What's that supposed to tell me?" he asked.

"That's my point, son." I slapped his shoulder. "Now, let's finish out here before I freeze in place." I could feel the work calm David, but the cold still drove us back to the house.

The whisky bottle was now on the table. Pamela and Howard were sitting next to each nursing glasses. The woman was making a fuss over the puppy, but Emily kept her distance, hanging tight to Gus's legs while he washed dishes.

"It's bad out there," I said. "We must have six inches already. Where's Morgan?"

"Upstairs," Gus said.

David walked to the table and poured himself a tall Scotch.

"Well, at least drink it slow," Howard said. "This is beautiful stuff. Aged in—" He stopped and turned to Pamela. "What kind of barrels?"

"Cherrywood."

"Cherrywood barrels." I could hear that Howard was tipsy.

To which David responded, "Fuck you."

Howard looked at Pamela, wide-eyed, then laughed. The woman laughed with him.

David walked out of the room.

Gus tossed his towel onto the counter and said, "That's it for me."

"You're not staying up for midnight?" Pamela asked.

"Nothing happens at midnight," Gus said. "Nothing that can't happen at ten o'clock or tomorrow morning. Good night, all."

"Good night, Gus," I said.

"Yeah, thanks for a great meal," Howard said.

"Thank you," from Pamela.

Gus left.

"You're not turning in, too, are you?" Howard asked me.

"As a matter of fact. This snow is going to make a lot of work for me in the morning, so I'm advised to get some sleep."

"Boo," said Pamela.

"Sorry," I said. "Good night."

I walked out, looked down the hall and saw that David's door was closed. I then climbed the stairs to find Morgan sitting on the bed. I sat beside her and asked what she was thinking about.

"Mother," she said.

I put my arm around her. "It's a tough time, these holidays."

"Poor David," she said.

"No kidding."

"Are they drunk yet?"

"Oh, yeah."

"I can't believe that you even know that man, much less that he's a close friend."

"Apparently, I don't know him." I got up, walked to the window, and watched the snow sift through the light of the vapor lamp on the barn. "Hopefully the snow will die down tonight, the roads will get plowed, and they'll be out of here tomorrow."

"Are you going back down there?" she asked.

"Do I look like I've just lost my mind? No, I say let's get all snuggly in bed and pretend that we're somewhere else."

"Like the Arctic?"

"That works."

The snow had done its job and made the world quiet. Momentarily. I awoke to shouting. Something like: "Fuck you!" and "Fuck you, too!" I sat up and looked at the clock; it was about midnight. Morgan awoke as well. She looked at me and tried to orient herself. She sat up.

"What's going on?" she asked.

"I think Howard and David are fighting."

Then Pamela's voice split the deeper ones, "Stop it!"

"Shut up," David shouted.

Then there was a silence.

I stepped to the door and opened it. Gus was standing inside his open door across the hall.

"Sounds bad," he said.

A door slammed. I wondered if I should go down. If David had just closed himself up in his room, then it might all be over. I certainly didn't want to hear anyone's side of anything right then.

"I guess that's it," I said.

Gus closed his door and I went back to bed.

"Come in here and get warm," Morgan said.

We started to kiss. I held Morgan and told her I loved her and I managed to get off her nightshirt. We had quiet, slow sex and then we lay in bed, watching the snow.

About a half-hour later there was a crash, breaking glass. Then a man's voice cried out.

"Good lord," I said. I threw back the covers and we got dressed. Gus followed us down the stairs and into the living room. The Scotch bottle was shattered on the floor and Howard was sitting on the sofa picking a shard of glass from his foot.

"What the Sam Hill?" Gus asked.

"I dropped the bottle," Howard said. "Stepped on some glass."

"Is it bad?" Pamela asked.

I looked down the hall and saw that David's door was open and the light was on. "Where's David?"

"He stormed out of here," Howard said. "He drank some more whisky and got drunk and just stormed out."

"When?" I asked.

"Awhile ago," he said.

Gus went into the kitchen and came back. "His jacket's in the mud room."

"Damnit!" I said. "Howard, why didn't you tell me!"

"So, he ran outside."

"It's ten-below out there." I looked at Morgan. "I'll look in the barns and you look around the outside of the house."

"What's going on?" Howard asked, beginning to understand that the situation was dire. He tried to focus on me through his drunkenness.

"Your son is out there with no coat and no boots, man." I turned to Gus. "Make some coffee and try to sober them up."

I pulled on my boots and parka and went out to the barns. I went through both twice and saw no sign of him. As I trotted back to the house I saw that the south gate was swinging with the wind. The gate had been closed. I sprinted back to the house.

Morgan was back inside. She shook her head.

Howard was shaking now, not from the cold, but from the realization of what had happened.

"Gus, I want you and Morgan to take the Jeep and drive up to the road, watch the sides. I'm going to ride south and search that way."

Morgan was terrified. I kissed her forehead.

By the time I had saddled the App and was traveling south toward the hills, an hour and a half had passed since the slamming of the door, plenty of time for hypothermia to set in, especially with the alcohol in him. I hoped that his youth and strength would help him. I also hoped that he was just yards from the gate and not miles. The beam of my flashlight was useless and so I moved slowly, trying to let my eyes adjust and hoping the horse could see better than I. I called out.

Finally my eyes were serving me and I could see the shapes of trees and tops of ridges. I rode faster. Ice formed in my moustache. I rode a few miles, feeling completely useless and helpless. Then the horse shied. I brought her back around and tried to see what had spooked her. I was in some trees and I shone my light at the bases of them. I dismounted and took a few steps.

There was David. He raised a weak hand into my light. He was stiff with cold. His clothes were wet. I was so scared I was hopping in place, wondering what to do, trying to get my bearings. I looked down the slope and spotted the shape of a fallen tree that I had seen many times; I'd used it as a mile marker. I was about four miles from my house. I was about a mile from the cave. I pulled David up and over my shoulder and eased him over the saddle. I walked the horse to the cave and brought her in out of the snow. The complete darkness made her jumpy and I tried to calm her. I got David down and checked him with my light. He was blue. His respiration was shallow. His clothes were soaked through. I put my hand on his stomach and it was ice cold. I wanted to build a fire, but I had no dry wood. I had to get the wet clothes away from his skin. I took him deeper into the cave, away from the opening and the wind. I took off his shirt and pants and socks and underwear; everything was soaked. Then I took off my clothes that were wet on the outside as well. I needed to use my body heat to warm him up. I needed to use the warmest thing I could find and that was my own 98.6 degrees. I pressed myself against him, rubbing his iced fingers in my hands, putting them in my armpits, blowing on them. He was shivering like no one I had ever seen, his teeth chattering, his eyes rolling back and showing white. "Come on, David, stay with me." I tried to warm his feet with my own. I thought that if he only lost some toes he'd be lucky. I kept talking to him. "It's going to be all right, son, hang on." I put my cheek on his.

He began to mutter things, more sounds than words. I tried to take that as a good sign. David moved his face to in front of me and he pressed his icy lips against mine. It took me a few seconds to realize it was a kiss. I had never been so confused. I let him kiss me, felt his shivering face soften to mine. I just wanted him warm, warmer. I couldn't pull away; I was trying to save his life.

ELEVEN

I COULD SEE a bit of gray on the wall of the cave. Morning was trying to press inside. David was asleep. Still, I couldn't see his face, but his breathing was strong. I turned on my light and studied him. I didn't shine the beam down to his feet; I wasn't ready for that. His stomach was no longer like ice. The constant temperature of the cave had saved both of us. I dressed and walked toward the entrance. It was early and I could see that the snow had stopped falling. The horse was standing calm just inside the mouth, her head low. I felt bad for having left her not only with the saddle but cinched tight. I released the girth and stroked her neck. I went back to David and woke him. He was groggy, but he sat up. He asked where he was.

"We're in a cave," I said.

"A cave?"

I imagined he felt his body and realized he was naked. "John, what's going on here?"

I turned my light on again. "You got drunk, had a fight with your father, ran out into the snow with sneakers and no jacket, I followed you into the woods, found you, and brought you here to get warm."

"I'm naked."

"You were soaked."

He was quiet while he sat there reconstructing the previous night, the flashlight illuminating the ceiling. "I got drunk," he said.

"I'll say."

"Where am I?" he asked again.

"I brought you into this cave to get warm. It was closer than the house. How do you feel?"

"I don't know." I thought I heard him start to cry. He grabbed his shirt from near him on the ground and pulled it over his lap. "My toes hurt."

"We'll have to look at them later," I said. "I've got to get you back to the house. You're going to wear my boots."

"I didn't wear boots?" he asked.

"Like I told you, you ran out in your sneakers." I was concerned that he still seemed disoriented.

"Shit."

I nodded. "It's relatively warm in here," I told him. "But it's freezing out there. We're lucky, at least the snow has stopped. There are some people worried to death about us."

"I'm really sorry."

"Don't worry about that now. Let's just get home. Get dressed. Put on my jacket as well."

"What about you?"

"I'm in better shape than you are, that's for sure. Just do like I said. Get dressed and meet me over by the entrance."

"My toes really hurt," he said.

I put the light on them. They were frostbitten, that was certain. I didn't know how badly. And since I didn't know, it was unclear to me whether I should try to thaw them out or leave them alone. I took off my socks. "Here put these on. Yours are still wet."

"What about you?"

"I'll wear your sneakers. Now, hurry up."

I was tightening the cinch when he joined me. He could barely walk. The front of his clothes were open.

"I can't do the buttons," he said. "My fingers hurt."

I fastened up his trousers, shirt, and jacket.

I stuck a sneakered foot in the stirrup, thankful that his feet were slightly larger than mine, climbed up into the saddle, and then leaned down to help him onto the horse behind me. He was staring at my eyes and I was fairly sure he was remembering having kissed me.

"Come on, son, I've got to get you someplace warm, both of us someplace warm." He took my arm. "Put your foot in the stirrup," I said. I pulled him up. "We're not going to ride fast, but it's steep in places, so hold tight." His clasped his hands around my waist. I rubbed the app's neck. "Sorry, old girl."

We rode off. The sky was clear and the snow was deep in places. My bare feet in the sneakers were aching and I could only imagine what they would have felt like sunk down into the snow and what David's feet must have felt like. There was not much wind at first, but when we came around the last turn and started down the hill, a breeze tore through my shirt and reminded me of all sorts of things. I was sick with the fact that Morgan and Gus would be worried. I was concerned about the horse; I wanted to bring her into the house. I was concerned about David's fingers and toes. The cold air made my nipples as tight and painful as I had ever felt them. But now I could see the house and so some kind of end. "There's the house," I said.

David didn't respond. I could feel his breathing, but I couldn't tell whether he was asleep or unconscious. As much as I hated to, I asked the App to trot across the big meadow. She was huffing.

I hit the south gate and saw a sheriff's rig parked by the house. I called out and Morgan came blasting through the back door, calling out behind her for Gus. Gus and Bucky followed and they ran to us. Bucky and Gus took David down. He was just awake and again trying to get his bearings. They helped him into the house. Morgan helped me out of the saddle, hugged me tightly.

"Into the house," she said.

"The horse," I said. I loosened the girth.

"I'll take care of the horse," she said. "She can stand for a minute."

"Okay," I said. "She saved me, Morgan." I could feel that I was a little disoriented, too, that perhaps I was suffering from the onset of hypothermia. "Into the house," I said.

"Where are your boots?" she asked.

"The boy is wearing them."

Morgan helped me up the steps and in through the back door.

The house felt flat-out hot. But that was good. I knew that was good. My feet ached like mad as blood and feeling tried to creep back into them. Morgan took me into the living room and sat me in front of the stove.

"The horse," I said.

"Okay, I'll go out now." She stroked my face, her hand feeling so warm. "You rest."

"Make sure you get all the ice out of her feet. Get her legs good and warm and rub them down with liniment, put her in a closed stall, put a blanket on her, give her some grain."

Morgan patiently listened, almost smiling. "Okay, sweetie."

"Rub her ears a bit, the tips."

"All right."

I drifted off to sleep.

I awoke to voices. Zoe was lying with me on the sofa, her back to me. I stroked her fur and felt her breathing. Gus's doctor, a fat man named Pep Clayton, was standing not far from me talking to Morgan. I sat up and Zoe moved to the floor. Clayton and Morgan turned to me.

"Pep," I said.

"John."

"Am I dead or do I just feel like it?"

"You just feel like it." He put a hand on my face. "You're fine. You no doubt saved that young man's life."

I tried to stand, but felt weak. I noticed that my feet didn't ache. Someone had put thick socks on me.

The doctor put a hand on my shoulder and pressed me back into the sofa. "You need to rest."

"How's David?" I asked.

"He's resting in the other room," Morgan said.

"He could be worse," Clayton said. "He'll make it through this just fine."

"What about his feet?" I looked at Clayton's eyes.

"He'll lose a few nails, but no toes. His fingers are all right."
Clayton sat beside me. "How'd you make it through the night?"

"I took him into a cave. He was soaked and it was closer than the
house. It's warmer in there. His belly was like ice."

"He's pretty weak. He'll probably sleep for a while. I told his
father and Morgan that they have to keep him warm, massage his
limbs, keep the blood flowing."

"How's the horse?" I looked at Morgan.

She smiled at me. "The horse is fine."

"Is David asleep now?" I asked.

Morgan nodded.

Gus came into the room. "I'm glad to see you in one piece,"
he said.

"Me, too." I looked at the window and at the bright light outside.
"What time is it?"

"Nearly two," the doctor said.

"Two," I repeated. I was still trying to wrap my mind around all
that had happened. "Where's Howard?"

"He's pretty shaken up," Gus said. "He's sitting in there with David.
Pamela's in the kitchen. She's making soup, she says."

I looked at the fire in the stove. It was hissing and popping with a
new log. I reached down and rubbed Zoe's head.

"Well, I'll be going," Clayton said. "There's not much else for me
to do around here."

"Thanks for coming out here, Pep."

"I'll see you out," Morgan said and walked away with the doctor
toward the front door.

"Is Bucky here?" I asked Gus.

"No, once he saw you were both here, he left."

"Is he okay, Gus?"

"I think so," Gus said. "You want something to eat?"

"Not really. I'd like some tea."

"I'll get it." Gus stopped and looked at me for a couple seconds.
"You sure you're all right?"

I nodded. "Why?"

He shook his head. "Warm enough?"

"I'm good." I watched him walk away. I pushed myself to stand and made my way to David's room. Howard was sitting on a straight-backed chair beside the bed. David was bundled in blankets, one of them electric.

Howard quickly got up when he saw me. "God, John, I don't know how to thank you."

"How is he?"

"Good, I think. He looks awful, but the doctor was positive about everything. His toes are the worst."

I scratched at my head. My skin felt dry everywhere. I knew I needed to rest, but I really wanted a hot shower.

"I've never been so scared in my life," Howard said.

It was then that I realized I was angry with the man and not in a generous mood, because, without thinking, I said, "You're sober enough now to be scared."

Howard froze. He didn't know what to say. I couldn't imagine what I would have said had I been him.

"You drink like that all the time or was that just your party face?"

"John, Pamela and I—"

"Pamela and you what?"

"Pamela's young."

"And what's your excuse?"

"John, I—"

I stopped him. "Why is she here? Did you think David was going to want to meet her? What was that all about?" He tried to speak again. "Listen," I said, "I don't want to hear it right now. Maybe never, I don't know. I want your son to be well. I want him to see you sitting by that bed when he opens his eyes and I don't want Pamela in this room."

"You're being a little harsh," he said.

"A little harsh?" I asked. "I must be tired or you must be misreading me because I mean to be very harsh. I'm going to get some rest." With that I turned away from him and went into the kitchen.

Pamela was stirring her soup at the stove. Gus was just pouring the hot water into the mugs. Pamela was thankfully covered in a sweater.

"You're up," she said.

"Yes." I looked at her and she could see the fight still in my eyes and she shrank away slightly. "Pamela, you seem like a nice person. I don't have anything against you and I don't know much about you. But I'd like you to somehow find a way to leave this ranch, with or without Howard as soon as you can."

I don't know what I expected, but her reaction must have fallen within the range of my expectations, because I was not surprised when she ran out of the room, holding her face in her hands, weeping.

The coyote came to me and jumped up against my leg. I gave her head a pat and looked at the stump of her leg.

"You want milk?" Gus asked.

"No, thanks."

"Morgan's out checking on the horses."

"That's good."

Morgan stepped into the shower with me. I wanted to grab her and kiss her, but I was too wiped out. She rubbed my shoulders and then began to lather up my head with shampoo.

"That feels good," I said.

"I love your hair," she said.

"What's left of it," I said.

"You're crazy. You've got nothing but hair up here."

"Very funny."

"Gus told me what you said to Pamela."

"I feel a little bad about that," I said. I put my face to the spray to rinse my eyes of shampoo. "I suppose I was venting."

"I suppose."

"Is she still crying?"

"Probably. I don't know. I believe that Howard is getting ready to leave with her."

I nodded. It was not an unexpected turn. What else could he do? He was planning to marry the woman so he couldn't very well send her alone on her way. Still, I was hoping he'd stay around for David.

"You've been in here long enough," Morgan said. "Time to get out, eat something, and go to bed."

"Yes, doctor."

"First, I'm going down to talk to Howard."

"First, you're going to let me dry your body and get you dressed."

"If you insist."

The hot shower had cooled me off somewhat. I felt bad for what I'd said to Howard and Pamela, but still I thought it would be better if they left. I made my way downstairs and into the den where they were slowly packing.

"Howard, Pamela," I said. I considered apologizing.

Pamela said nothing, but she tugged at the bottom of her shirt that barely covered her navel. She stuffed a sweater into her bag.

"We'll be gone soon," Howard said, coolly.

"I'm sorry things worked out this way," I said.

"It's not your fault," Howard said. "It's certainly not your fault."

"Pamela, I didn't mean to hurt your feelings." My words might have been sincere, but they weren't true.

"Do you want your scarf in the bag or out?" she asked Howard.

"Out," he said.

I backed away, imagining that Howard's request was not merely a response to Pamela, but a command to me. I looked down the hall at David's door. I walked to it, waited a few seconds, then walked in. David was asleep but awoke as I stood there. I moved to the foot of his bed.

"Warm enough?" I asked.

"Too warm," he said.

I reached down and picked up the control for the electric blanket. It was set on ten. "Maybe Gus was planning to serve you for dinner. I think I can just turn this off now."

"Thank you," he said.

"You bet. How are you feeling?"

My toes still hurt," he said. "But not as much. I believe that's supposed to be a good sign. Gus told me that. Gus told me everything. I'm sorry."

I just looked at him, not sure what he was talking about. "Sorry?"

"Sorry for running out like a stupid child and causing everybody to worry." He closed his eyes for a second. "Sorry I made you come out there and have to save me. I feel like such a jerk."

"Hey, you would have come out after me," I said. "You were upset. That's understandable. And apparently, you shouldn't drink."

"I knew that before."

"Your father's packing to leave," I told him.

"Good."

"Well, you get some more rest. I'm going to do the same thing."

In the kitchen, the puppy was bouncing around, roughhousing with Zoe. The little girl growled, leaned back, and lurched forward. I looked over at Gus and Morgan sitting at the table.

"Somebody please turn the puppy over," I said.

"She's only playing," Morgan said.

"Gus, flip her over."

Gus got up, walked to the coyote, kneeled down and flipped her onto her back. Emily kicked, twisted and tried to reach over his hand to bite him.

"Hold her until she doesn't squirm," I said.

He did. The coyote surrendered, became soft under Gus's hand and he slowly let her up.

"Thank you," I said.

"Are you all right?" Morgan asked, a kind of accusation.

I closed my eyes briefly, then opened them. "I'm fine. I'm sorry, you two. I'm just tired and worried about everything too much."

"No, you were right about Emily," Gus said. "I've been lazy about the training. I need to turn her over more and take her food away like you told me."

"Gus, you're doing fine. Really."

Morgan asked me if I wanted tea.

"Is there any coffee?"

"I'll make some," Gus said. He opened the cupboard and took down the coffee beans.

"I just looked in on David. He was awake. He appears to be in pretty good shape."

Morgan nodded and sipped her tea. "Did you tell him that his father is leaving?" she asked.

"I did. The news didn't seem to bother him too much. I guess that's a good thing. Where is Howard?"

"Having a drink?" Gus said, sarcastically.

"No, actually, he's preparing to leave," Howard said from the doorway.

Gus turned to the counter and ran the grinder for several seconds, then a couple more seconds.

"I'm sorry all this happened," I said. It was an expression of dismay and not an apology.

"Yeah, me, too," Howard said, softly. Neither was he apologizing. He had settled into anger; his jaw was fixed. He tossed a glance back to Pamela who hovered at his shoulder.

"Have a good trip," Gus said. "The roads can be slippery."

"It was nice meeting you," Morgan said, seeming to suck the statement back in once it was out.

Howard didn't say anything. What could he say? I followed them to the front door where they had already placed their bags. I reached out to shake Howard's hand and he reluctantly took it.

"We'll talk soon," I lied.

TWELVE

DAVID'S LIMP was still noticeable, but he claimed to feel little pain. He had stopped taking the pain medication prescribed by the doctor and after a few trips into town to have his toes examined, he was satisfied or at least convinced that he was fine, however repulsed he was by his toes' appearance, the missing nails and the off color. He was well enough to have a few more lessons on horseback and in all seemed in good spirits. We hadn't again talked about that night in the cave and nearly three weeks had gone by.

Gus had taken to sleeping late regularly. He'd appear at about eight-thirty, sit with Morgan, and have coffee and toast. I was glad Morgan was there for him.

I'd managed to get myself back on my training schedule. A couple of young colts and a filly had been dropped off. Felony was almost ready for pick up. After giving Duncan Camp's daughter a couple of lessons on him, I was feeling confident about letting him go. And finally, I'd taken to riding Pest, the mule. He was a good ride, if a tad small for me, but he was stout and smart, good on the steep and liked the activity. When I rode him, he was likely to stay put in his stall or a paddock longer.

Morgan and I rode every day at midday, leaving David to muck the stalls and have lunch with Gus. One day we rode out past the cave and looked down at the desert. The weather had turned unseasonably warm, as Weather Wally liked to say, and we had taken off our jackets. Morgan, sitting on her horse Square, was slightly above me on Pest.

"I could get used to this," Morgan said.

"Used to what?" We were crossing the high meadow on way back.

"Being above you like this."

"Well, when you put it like that."

"John, do you think David likes me?"

"Sure," I said. "Why do you ask that?"

"He's always been quiet around me, but lately, I don't know. He's even been different around you."

I nodded. "That whole thing with his father must have been plenty embarrassing."

"Yeah. And I suppose all his toes do is remind him."

As we rode back, I thought about David. It was stupid that his kissing me while delirious should have made either of us feel strange, but of course it did. I tried to convince myself that I was not bothered by having been kissed by a man. Maybe I tried too hard, as my trying made me feel as weird as the kiss. I cared for David. I might have said like a son, but he wasn't my son. Before the kiss, I might have admitted to someone who asked that I loved him. Now, that word, that sentiment, was muddied. The part about the kiss that bothered me was that it did not feel bad, it was an expression of affection and I could feel affection. But it also was not that, as it was offered in blindness, in the dark of the cave and in the confusion of David's disorienting condition.

"What are you thinking about?" Morgan asked.

"Nothing," I said. I was glad I was not sitting on Felony at that moment. I'd have been halfway to town.

"You were thinking something."

"I was thinking that I'd be a little lost without you here," I said, which was true, but it wasn't what I was thinking. "I never thought I'd need anyone again, but I need you. Is that okay?"

"That's wonderful, John Hunt," she said.

At dinner that night we discussed the goings-on near the reservation. Morgan was rightly worried and I was trying to play it down without playing it down. Gus pushed his plate of nearly untouched salad to the center and leaned back.

"I'll tell you one thing," he said. "I don't blame White Buffalo for not trusting the sheriff. What's his name? Fucky?"

"Gus," Morgan said. "Such language. Why the hell would you say some shit like that?"

Gus roared. David laughed as well and that was good to see.

"Why don't you trust him?" I asked.

"He's a cop for one thing." He looked down at the floor, scratched the coyote's ear. "And he wears that holster with no thumb-break snap."

"What's that?" David asked.

"It's a piece of leather that wraps over the trigger and keeps the pistol in the holster," I said.

"He thinks he's a damn cowboy riding the range looking for desperadoes. He's gonna mess around and shoot his own foot off."

I nodded. I'd always considered Bucky to be all right, but I trusted Gus's instincts and I couldn't dismiss them out of hand.

"I've never shot a gun," David said.

"That's not a bad thing," I said. "Nothing will get somebody shot faster than a gun."

Gus drank some water and cleared his throat. "Guns ain't evil," he said. "They're bad, but they're not evil. The problem is that guns are easy. Any idiot can use one and any idiot can feel tough with one. I suppose guns are fine for hunting."

"I don't think I would be able to kill an animal," David said.

"Somebody's got to do it," Gus said. "Killing isn't hard. It only takes a second. It's what comes after that's hard." He paused. "Sometimes."

We sat around in a silent stew for a bit. Then I said, "Well, I say we go into the other room and play Scrabble and exercise some of those killer instincts."

"You bet," Morgan said.

"Right after David and I go move a couple hundred pounds of horseshit."

In the barn, David and I set to work in different areas. The clear night had become chilly and we wanted to get back inside. I stopped as I wheeled a cart of manure past the stall David was cleaning. I silently watched.

David knew I was there, but said nothing as he forked the last of the droppings into the bucket. Then he stood straight and said, "Gus really doesn't like the sheriff."

"No, he really doesn't," I said.

"Does this stuff make you nervous? The dead cows and everything."

"Of course it does."

"You don't seem nervous," he said.

I shrugged. "Seeming nervous and being nervous are different things."

"To tell the truth, I'm scared."

"So is Morgan," I said. "So am I. I don't know about Gus. He's seen a lot. I still don't know what scares him."

"Is that it?" David asked. He was talking about what there was to do with the horses.

"I suppose it is."

The next morning, after chores and breakfast, David and I were in the flatbed truck on our way into town for hay and people food. We made the big curve and I noted that the sky was beginning to threaten again. I glanced over at David. He was looking out the window.

"You know, we haven't talked about it," I said.

"About what?"

"That night in the cave. You think we ought to try?" I down shifted as we headed down the grade.

"I don't know what there is to say."

"I feel like it's put some distance between us," I said. "You were in pretty bad shape that night."

"I know I was. Like I said, I'm sorry about everything."

"I'm not asking for an apology," I said.

"But I am sorry. I'm sorry I kissed you." Saying it was hard for him. And, to tell the truth, it was hard for me to hear. "Did it make you feel weird?" It was not so much a question as a lashing out.

"I suppose it did," I said. "I'd never kissed a man before."

He just looked at me.

"What is it?"

"Did you feel anything when we kissed?"

"What are you talking about?"

"Did you feel anything?" he asked again.

"You were in bad shape," I said and realized I was repeating my-self. "No, I didn't feel anything. I felt your lips and I felt you shiv-ering and I felt like you might die. Besides, you were out of it and didn't know what you were doing."

"Does that make you feel better about it?" he asked.

"It doesn't make me feel one way or another," I told him. "Listen, I'm not trying to fight you about this. I just thought we should talk about it."

"Why?"

"Now, I'm sorry I brought it up. I don't know why." I was just sick that I'd said anything. "David, you've become my friend. I want you to stay my friend."

"You want me to promise I won't kiss you again?"

"Maybe we should just drop this."

"Maybe we should," he said.

"To hell with that." He'd put me on the prod. "Listen, kid, I don't care that you kissed me. You're alive, that's what I was thinking about. I simply don't like the silence you've been dishing out. It makes me feel bad. But more importantly, it makes Morgan feel bad. If you can't get it together, perhaps you should consider going back to Chicago."

Those words hung there in the air for a few minutes. We rolled along the flat stretch that led into town.

"I'm sorry," he said.

"Stop apologizing, goddamnit."

"I'm attracted to you."

I sighed. "Jesus, David, that's not what I'm looking to hear right now. That's not getting us back to where we were."

"I'm just being honest."

"Son, that's beautiful and all that, but really. I mean, I'm flattered, but really."

"It's not like I expect anything from you." His voice was surprisingly steady.

"Well, that's good."

"Like I said, I'm just being—"

"Honest, I know. Listen, I'm flattered as all hell, but you know what I have to say here, so I won't even bother."

"I know."

I turned on the radio. We drove past the goddamn Wal-Mart.

"I want you to be my friend," David said. "I trust you."

"I appreciate that," I told him.

"I don't want to go back to Chicago yet." He was staring at me.

"You don't have to leave, son."

David laughed. "You know what's funny. When you call me son, I almost believe it. At least, it sounds like it makes sense. My own father only called me son when he was angry and even then it sounded strange in his mouth."

"Life's weird, isn't it?"

"Are we friends?" he asked.

"Yes, we are."

I introduced David to Myra at the feed store and they seemed to hit it off right away. At least David appeared to enjoy the way Myra referred to me as "Ugly Over There." We ran into Duncan Camp and I told him he could come pick up Felony whenever he wanted.

"You've done a good job with him." Camp was nursing a Styrofoam cup of coffee. "This man knows horses," he said to David.

"He should," Myra said. "He looks like one."

"Thank you, ma'am," I said.

"So, how do you like working for Mr. Hunt?" Camp asked David.

"I like it."

"Because if you get tired of him, you're welcome over at my place. I've got a ton of work that needs doing."

"I'll keep that in mind," David said.

Duncan Camp walked out to the truck with us and followed me around to the driver's side. "You okay?" he asked.

"Yeah, why?"

"Bucky told me about what happened out at White Buffalo's place."

"Morgan's nervous."

"I'll bet," he said.

"We're just keeping our eyes open," I said. "What else can we do?"

At the market, I paused to talk to Kent Hollis, the librarian, and his wife while David pushed the cart with the groceries across the parking lot to the truck. They both looked tired and I got the impression that Mrs. Hollis's health was not so good.

"We heard about the hate crimes," Hollis said.

"Well, you know, people are worse than anybody," I said.

Mrs. Hollis laughed, then coughed. Hollis leaned over her chair to see to her. She waved him off.

"Seems like all anybody can talk about today," I said. I watched as David opened the passenger side and pulled forward the seat.

"I haven't seen you in the library lately," Hollis said. "I miss your once-a-week visit."

"I've been busy. My friend's son is staying with me for a while." I indicated David with a nod.

"It's going to snow, Kent," Mrs. Hollis said.

"I think you're right, Mrs. Hollis," I said.

"Well, we'd better get on." Hollis shook my hand. "We don't like being out in bad weather with the chair and all."

"I don't like being out in it either," I told them. "You two stay warm and healthy."

David had just deposited the cart in the rack in the middle of the lot and was walking back to the truck, when the BMW skidded to a stop near him. I started to trot, then slowed to a fast walk. David walked around the car, but the two men inside stepped out. One of the men was the one whose nose I'd broken. I'd never seen the other. I slowed to a normal walk when I saw that David was pointing up the street. Before I got there the car was pulling away.

"What was that all about?" I asked.

"They wanted to know where the diner is."

"Really." I said. It wasn't a question.

"Yeah, so I told them."

"Do you remember that skinny guy?" I asked.

"Yeah, he's the one who picked the fight with Robert and me." David climbed into the truck.

I walked around and got behind the wheel. "Pretty weird, eh?" I said.

David nodded.

"I've got a headache. You think you can drive this beast?"

"I can drive it."

I got out and walked around while David slid across the seat.

"I'm just going to close my eyes. It's not fancy, but we've got a load, so be sure to downshift and save the brakes. Don't go over fifty-five and don't wake me with any sudden collisions."

"Okay," he laughed.

I closed my eyes.

I did manage to drift off to sleep and I came to with the knowledge that I was not driving and so I awoke with a start. I looked over at David and he was looking at me.

"Keep your eyes on the road," I said.

"Bad dream?" he asked.

"I guess." I sat up and realized we were just a couple of miles from the road to my place. I'd slept for quite a while. "Good job," I told him.

"Piece of cake." He turned onto the dirt road and bounced with the ruts. "Sorry."

"It's hard to miss them," I said. "The county snowplows to the fork. They take a decent dirt lane and make sure it complies with the state washboard code."

"They do a good job."

"It's a kidney buster, but at least it's a little better with a full load." It started to rain.

"That should make it better," I said.

David laughed.

"Just go slow down the hill."

There were two pickups parked in front of the house. Their presence caused me to sit straight.

"Company?" David asked.

"Apparently."

Before I could get worried, Daniel White Buffalo stepped out onto the porch with Gus and two other men. I got out and told David to drive the truck into the barn to get the hay out of the rain. I walked to the porch.

"Daniel, what are you doing way out here?" I said in the way of a greeting.

"Wanted to check your reservation for a change." He pointed to the other men with a nod. "You know Wilbert Monday. And this here is Elvis Two Horses."

"Wilbert. Nice to meet you, Elvis."

"We been talking to your uncle," Daniel said. "He says you're crazy."

"It's not a secret," I said. "What's up?" I was on the porch with them now. "More dead cattle?"

"No dead cows," Daniel said. "Just weird things. Tell him, Wilbert."

Wilbert looked at Daniel, then at me. He was a lean man with his mother's hard eyes. His voice was somewhat high and appeared to come from someone else. "I was over in the Owl Creeks looking for cows," he said. Then after a long pause, "I saw two figures in the hills."

"So?" I said.

"Nobody we know will go into the Owl Creeks," Elvis Two Horses said.

"You were over there?" I said to Wilbert.

"Like I said, I was looking for cows."

"Maybe they were looking for cows," I said.

Wilbert lit a cigarette. "Who looks for cows on foot?"

I saw David walking from the barn toward me. I called to him. "David, check all the water while you're out there." He made an exaggerated pivot and walked away. "So, why are you here?" I asked again.

"We want you to talk to the sheriff," Daniel said.

"And tell him that Wilbert saw two men walking through the hills?"

Gus cleared his throat. "I tried to tell them that Fucky Bucky was going to be of no help to them or us."

"Why me?" I asked.

"If it comes from just us nobody listens," Daniel said.

"What makes you think that anyone will listen to me?"

"I don't know," Daniel said.

"Things ain't right," Elvis Two Horses said.

"What do you want me to say to him, the sheriff?" I asked.

"I don't know," Daniel said again.

I looked up at the gray sky. The rain had stalled. "I'll give him a call."

I shook their hands and watched as they left, Daniel in one truck, the other two in the other. "How did I get elected club president?" I asked.

"I have to apologize for something," Gus said, changing the subject.

"What's that?"

"I forgot to ask you to pick up my medicine at the pharmacy."

"That's okay, Gus. You need it today?"

"I'll need it tomorrow morning."

"I'll drive in now and get it. Where's Morgan?"

"She saddled her horse and rode out. About a half-hour ago." David walked toward us.

"I've got to make another run into town," I said. "Want to ride along?"

"I forgot about my damn medicine," Gus said.

"You've got work to do," David said. "I'll go. I know the way there and back. If I can drive that truck, I can drive the Jeep."

I suddenly felt like an overprotective father. I didn't want to say yes, but I didn't know why. "That would be good, David," I said. "I appreciate it. That'll give me time to work the animals I didn't work yesterday."

"Thanks, youngblood," Gus said. "I'll grab the prescription." Gus ducked into the house.

"At least the rain gave up," I said.

David looked at the sky, but said nothing.

Gus poured hot water into our mugs.

I stood at the window and watched my mule walk back into the barn. "What do they expect me to do?" I asked.

"They're just scared. They think you can talk to the sheriff."

"Why do they think that?" I asked.

"Because you don't hate him," Gus said. He sat down at the table and rubbed his knee. "Grab the honey over there."

I grabbed the honey pot and put it down in front of him, walked back to the window and looked out.

"They think you trust the sheriff."

"Hmmm," I said.

"Do you?"

"Why shouldn't I?" I felt on the defensive. I felt that admitting trusting the sheriff was admitting to stupidity or naïveté. Worse, I had the sense that my trusting him suggested a kind of betrayal, but I didn't know of whom.

To my question, Gus merely offered a shrug.

Morgan rode her horse at a walk through the gate, leaned over and closed it. She dismounted at the hitching post by the barn and looked up at the window. I waved to her. She tipped her helmet.

"Morgan's back," I told Gus.

"Good." He picked up Emily and held her in his lap.

I left the old man in the kitchen and walked across the yard.

"Hey, there," she said.

"You want to get hitched?" I asked.

"You bet." She gave me a kiss.

"Nice ride?"

"It's beautiful out."

"It's perfect horse weather," I said. I'm going to work those colts, then put Felony through his paces another time."

"Where's David?" Morgan asked.

"He drove into town for Gus's medicine."

"Oh, really," she said.

"What's that supposed to mean?" I asked.

"Is there something I should know about?" she asked. She undid the cinch and let the girth swing under the horse. "Is there something between you two?"

"I don't know what you mean."

"John, I've known you for a long time. I know when you're not telling me something and you're not telling me something. Ever since that night he ran off and almost got himself killed you've been acting funny."

"Maybe so," I said. "I guess I'm worried about him. I feel bad that all that grizzly stuff that happened with his father here and now I wonder why he's here."

"He has a crush on you," she said.

"I know," I said. "It makes me uncomfortable."

"Me, too," she said.

"I don't know what to do about it. Should I say something?"

She unhooked the horse's breastplate, then walked around to re-move the saddle from the off side the way she always did. Her saddle was heavy and she'd always pull it off and swing it over the post in one motion. She came back to me, took the bridle from my hand and kissed my chin. "I don't know what you should say, either," she said. "I've got a crush on you; why shouldn't he?"

I nodded.

"Besides, he's not your type," she said.

"Too tall?"

"No, he's emotional." She untied her horse. "So, you let him drive into town alone. Big step."

"He's twenty years old."

"Yeah, yeah." I followed her as she led Square to his stall. "He doesn't have much use for me, I can tell you that. I don't think he dislikes me, but I'm in the way, if you know what I mean."

Once Morgan had closed the stall door, I put my arms around her. "I have to admit David's pretty cute, but he's too young for me, don't you think? And then there's the fact that he's a man."

"I'm being silly," she said.

I kissed her. "You're not being silly. For some reason, I'm over-attentive to the kid. I like him a lot."

"Did something happen that night?" she asked.

I looked at Morgan's eyes and I couldn't find it in myself to lie or maybe it's that I didn't believe I could lie believably. "There was one thing. He was soaking wet, so I had to undress him. I held him close, trying to keep him warm and he kissed me."

"He kissed you," she repeated.

I nodded. "On the mouth. Then he passed out again. He remem-bers doing it and he's embarrassed by it."

"What was it like?" Morgan asked. I could identify her tone.

"What do you mean?"

"Did it feel good?"

"It didn't feel like anything," I said. I thought that perhaps I was lying, that maybe the kiss had felt in some way good. "I was scared he was going to die."

We stood there, awkwardly silent.

"I love you, Morgan."

She kissed me. She turned away and started out of the barn and I could tell we still had a problem.

"Morgan," I called to her.

She stopped, but did not turn to face me. "What?" It came out as an uncharacteristic bark.

"What am I supposed to say?"

"You're not supposed to say anything."

"I didn't do anything," I said.

"I know you didn't, John." She turned and looked at my eyes. "You've been perfect. You're always perfect. You take care of all of us perfectly. Now, I don't want to talk about this anymore. Is that all right?"

The rain was falling steadily now. It was five-thirty and dark and still there was no sign of the Jeep coming down the hill toward the house. I'd been checking the window for a couple hours and before that I'd been stepping out of the barn to watch the lane. Morgan brought me some tea.

"I'm sure he's all right," she said.

"Come on, let's go for a drive," I said. "Gus, you stay here in case he comes back."

"You got it."

"I'll drive, you look," Morgan said.

We put on our jackets and walked out to Morgan's car. Morgan was shaking and not because she was cold.

We drove all the way to town. The pharmacist told us that David had been there hours ago. I used his phone to call Gus. David had

not shown up. We drove the streets of town. I was behind the wheel now. We checked the grocery parking lot and the lots of the Wal-Mart, the motels, and the restaurants. I parked in front of the sheriff's office.

"John?" Morgan said.

"I don't know, honey. Let's see if we can get some other people on the road with us."

Inside, Hanks listened to me and told me that no accidents had been reported. I used his phone to get another no-show report from Gus. He had a dispatcher call another deputy and ask him to drive the road to my place.

"Thanks," I said.

"Come on," Morgan said to me and pulled me toward the door.

"I'll call you if I hear anything," Hanks said.

Morgan and I walked out and got back into her car. I was again behind the wheel, but I didn't start the Jeep. "I can't believe this is happening again," I said. The rain was falling less hard.

Morgan reached over and touched my hand.

"I love you so much," I said.

"I know you do, John. I love you, too."

"Where is he?"

THIRTEEN

TO SAY THAT I couldn't believe the current set of circumstances was an understatement. Morgan and Gus took turns convincing me, or trying to convince me that I was not to blame for having let David drive into town alone. After driving back and forth between town twice, Morgan and I stapled ourselves to the house and waited for the phone to ring. Gus fell asleep on the sofa and Morgan covered him with a blanket. Then she fell asleep on the big chair in front of the stove. I paced, let the dogs out a couple times, and finally watched the sunrise. At first light I called the sheriff and learned that nothing had been learned.

"So, what now?" I asked Bucky.

"I called the Highway Patrol and they're supposed to be sending an investigator," he said.

"What should I do?"

"I don't know, John. We're still out there driving the roads. All the roads we can anyway."

"Thanks." I hung up and looked in on Gus and Morgan. They were still asleep. I gently woke Morgan to tell her I was going to feed the horses.

"Okay," she said. "Do you want me to make breakfast?" She was only half awake.

"No, you sleep some more."

I left the house and went about the chores. My mind kept turning to the thugs in the BMW. How could I not think of them? The next time I talked to the sheriff I would mention them, ask if anything was known about them. I wondered if I should call Howard or

David's mother. That thought made me feel as if I was giving into the worst notions and I felt bad, like I was giving up on the boy. Thinking of this made no sense to me and I became disoriented. I sat and watched the three-legged coyote splash after a stick in the mud.

I didn't know what to do. I couldn't very well go about my daily business as if nothing was wrong. I didn't know where else to drive and look. And I didn't see myself going into town and making myself a troublesome and unwanted fixture at the sheriff's office. I cleaned half the stalls and went back to the house.

Morgan had coffee waiting and was starting breakfast when I walked into the kitchen. Had there been any word she would have spoken up immediately, so I didn't ask.

"What's the weather like?" she wanted to know.

"I think we're done with the rain," I said. "It's not terribly cold."

"That's good."

"Is Gus still asleep?" I asked.

"He's in the shower. You know, he's looks really tired."

I nodded. I opened the door and let the dogs in. They were wet and muddy, but I didn't care. The phone rang. Morgan watched me while I picked up. It was Daniel White Buffalo.

"Daniel," I said.

"Hey, I heard about your friend," he said.

"What did you hear?" I could hardly feel myself breathing.

"One of the deputies drove by last night, said he was missing."

"Yeah, he's driving my Jeep," I said.

"We'll keep our eyes open over here."

"Thanks, Daniel."

We sat stupidly silent on the phone for a few seconds. "Okay, Daniel. Thanks."

"You bet."

I hung up.

The phone rang again and this time it was Bucky. Morgan came and stood close to me while I talked to him.

"John, I've got a guy from the Highway Patrol and he'd like you to come talk to him."

"Okay. Anything yet?"

"No, nothing. Can you come in now?"

"I'll be there in an hour."

"We've looked just about everywhere," the sheriff said. "We've got a plane up right now."

"That's good, I guess. I'll be right there." I hung up and looked at Morgan. "I'm going in to talk to the Highway Patrol."

"You want to eat something first?" Morgan asked.

"I can't eat. I'm going to go wash my face, then head into town."

"I'll stay by the phone," Morgan said.

The drive into town felt exceptionally long and I didn't even notice the view of the valley as I made the big curve. Though my hands weren't shaking, I wouldn't have been surprised to find them so. The traffic in town was a little heavier than usual; I had to sit at one light through three changes before I could get past it. But it was while I was idling there that I saw the BMW parked in the Wal-Mart lot. My thought was to go into the store and find the men, but I didn't know what I'd say. Instead, I drove on to Bucky's office and parked the pickup in a diagonal space in front of the town square.

Bucky introduced me to a tall man with a handlebar mustache. His name was Reg McCormack. He wore expensive Western boots and an easy manner. His handshake was cold, limp.

"Tell me about your friend," he said.

"He's about six feet tall, one-sixty maybe, twenty years old, light brown hair. He's white. He was driving my Jeep."

"Any reason he drove into town alone?"

"We'd just come back from picking up hay and we found out my uncle had forgotten to have us pick up his medicine," I said.

"Whose idea was it that he drive?" McCormack asked.

I looked at Bucky, then answered, "He offered to drive in." I didn't like the tone of his questions.

"How long was he gone before you became concerned?"

"It was getting dark," I said, thinking. "Three hours, I guess, maybe a little longer. He'd never driven in alone before."

"Why was that?"

I shrugged. "Hey, why all the questions?"

"I have to ask them, Mr. Hunt."

"Listen, my friend's kid is out there somewhere, probably in trouble."

"Your friend's kid?"

"Yes, David is the son of an old college friend."

"I understand you had some trouble with the boy before," McCormack said. "A deputy had to drive out to your ranch?"

"He got lost in the woods, but I found him."

"So, he has a habit of going missing," the man said.

"I wouldn't say that," I said. "He was driving this time. Last time he'd had words with his father and ran out of the house drunk."

"Was he drunk this time?"

"No, he wasn't."

"He wasn't drunk when he left your place," McCormack said. "Was he drunk when he left town to head back?"

"I think he wasn't," I said.

"But you're not sure."

I was starting to get mad, but I sucked it in. "A twenty-year-old kid is out there somewhere, maybe pinned under a Jeep, and we're playing games in here. You should be talking to the thugs in town who are running around shooting cattle and writing the word *nigger* in the snow with blood."

"I will," McCormack said, unfazed.

"No, really, these guys have tried to pick fights with David on a couple of occasions," I said. "They drive a BMW."

"Why would they want to fight David?" he asked.

"They don't like the fact that he's a homosexual."

"How do you feel about that fact?"

I stared at McCormack for several seconds, then stood. "Bucky, this is getting us nowhere. You've seen the guys I'm talking about. Find them and ask them some questions. In the meantime, I'm going to drive the same roads for the seventh and eighth times trying to find David."

"I'm trying to help, Mr. Hunt," McCormack said.

I nodded. "Then talk to the guys in the BMW."

As I was walking through the main office, I became aware of a bustle of activity. I paused and watched, listened. Bucky came out of his office.

"Hanks found your Jeep," he said.

The vehicle was parked, almost neatly, about twenty miles off the main highway on an undeveloped road into the Red Desert, about thirty miles west and south of my place. I hadn't found it because I was looking between my place and town. I used the station phone to call my house and then followed Bucky and McCormack. The Jeep had been spotted from the air and there apparently was no sign of David. As I drove I felt as if progress was being made, but that none of it sounded at all good. Now, my hands were shaking.

Hanks was standing at the rear of the Jeep when we arrived and he had admittedly done little more than wait. The sheriff department's plane was still circling. The sheriff, McCormack, and I all walked around the vehicle like it might say something. McCormack looked the most closely, asking us to keep our distance.

"We'll need to go over it," McCormack said.

"Team's on the way," Hanks told him.

McCormack stood next to me. "Your rig?"

I nodded. "Can you tell anything?"

"There's a small, white, paper bag on the seat," Hanks said.

"Probably my uncle's medicine," I said.

We stood around while clouds collected over us. The plane left. More men arrived and I watched as they examined the Jeep. I looked down the deeply rutted dirt path and wondered how far it went into the desert. I tried to get my bearings by looking at the hills and the distant butte. I realized I wasn't that far from where I'd found the coyote. We were perhaps only ten miles south of that place.

McCormack came back to me. "You ever been here before?"

I shook my head.

"Your friend didn't say anything to you before he left?"

"He said, 'See you later.'"

"I'm just trying to help," he said.

"Yeah, fuck you," I said. That was unlike me, but I wasn't feeling much like myself. I turned and walked toward my truck.

"Where are you going?"

"I'm going to look for my friend," I said. I turned and walked back to him. "My uncle needs his medicine."

McCormack called to one the investigators. "Let him have the bag."

I took the medicine and left.

As I drove away, I glanced into my mirror and watched McCormack watching me leave. I knew that there was no way for him to implicate me in David's disappearance, but still I was insulted. I didn't know what to do. I would go home, give Gus his medicine, tell him and Morgan about the Jeep, and then stare at the telephone. I had to call Howard and David's mother, Sylvia.

The ruts of the trail threw me about pretty roughly. I hadn't felt it on the way out, perhaps because of adrenaline or shock. But now every trough and hole bounced the truck. One thing was certain, no BMW had come along this road. That thought slightly depressed me, because the thugs were the only notion I had about what might have happened.

When I arrived at the house I didn't know how to let Gus and Morgan see me from the porch, I became self-conscious about my gestures. If I shook my head, they might take it to mean that David was found dead. If I didn't, they'd assume the same thing. A shrug would have been incomprehensible. So, when I set the brake and climbed out of the truck, I shouted, "Nothing!" That was more than a assessment of what was known, it was a statement of what I was feeling. I was

numb with shock, too confused to admit my fear and somewhere
the anger and guilt and anger about feeling guilty.

I tossed Gus his medicine and he caught it. "They found the
Jeep," I said. "Abandoned in the desert."

"Oh, John." Morgan embraced me.

I put my hand to the small of her back, but didn't find the strength
to pull her close.

"What now?" Gus said.

And what a good question that was. I looked at the old man. "I
don't know, Gus. I don't know." I looked at the mountains, then felt
that the air was turning colder. "I'm going to call Howard. Then I'm
going to drown myself in the shower. Then I'm going back out to look
for David." I stopped and looked at both of them. Morgan's eyes were
red from lack of sleep and Gus was as drawn looking as I had ever
seen him. "How are you two?"

Gus nodded.

"We all need rest," Morgan said. Then, "This is all so unreal."

You watch the news and see stories about awful accidents and missing loved ones and it seems so distant, like it isn't real and then when
it happens to you, it doesn't seem real. I kept expecting David to
walk into the study where I was sitting, then I entertained thoughts
that there was no David, that I had made him up. I pulled my rifle
from the cabinet and set the cleaning supplies on the desk. I looked
at the phone, knowing I would use it. I then looked at the rifle in my
lap and had a feeling that I would be using it as well.

I opened my book, found Howard's number and dialed.

"Howard, it's John."

"Hey, I was going to give you a call."

"Howard, there's a problem here."

Howard was silent at the other end.

"David is missing."

"What do you mean by 'missing'?"

"We can't find him." Before he launched into reasonable, sensible and appropriate questions, I continued, "He drove into town and didn't come back. He went in to pick up a prescription for Gus. The police just found the Jeep he was driving abandoned out in the desert."

Howard was still silent.

"I don't know what to say. I've been out searching. They found the Jeep by air. As far as I know there was no sign of anything strange or unusual. But I haven't talked to the sheriff for a couple of hours."

"Missing? Was there blood?" The question made sense, still it ran cold through me. "Was there any blood?"

"I don't know," I said. "I didn't see any. I'm so sorry, Howard."

"What should I do?" His question hung in the wires between us. It wasn't really directed at me, but then it was.

"I don't know. I'm going out to search more. I don't know where to look, but I'll look."

"I'll call Sylvia," he said.

"Okay. I'm sorry, Howard."

"You think he's okay?" he asked.

"I hope so. I hope so."

"I'll call you later."

I hung up and blew out a long breath that shook my lower lip and realized my teeth were chattering. I placed my head down on my arms on top of my desk and soon fell asleep.

In my dream, Susie was sewing at a treadle machine, something she never did, in fact, she didn't own one. But there she was, her booted foot marking an exact rhythm. I had been working outside. I was sweating and for some reason I had not removed my jacket or my filthy boots. She was intent on her activity and when I asked her what she was making, she said,

"It's a patch quilt, but it has no pieces."

"Then how can it be a patch quilt?" I asked.

She stopped sewing and glared up at me. "Why do you always have to be so critical of me?"

"I'm sorry," I said. "I guess I just don't understand."

"There's a lot you don't understand." Her foot started again and she began to push and pull the fabric beneath the needle. "You think I don't know."

"I think you don't know what?"

"I see the look in your eyes," she said.

I didn't know what she was talking about, but I felt pressed to make her feel right. "Is the quilt a gift for someone?" I asked.

She didn't answer me, didn't look up, kept sewing.

"It looks like it's going to be beautiful."

"Do you love him?"

"Who?"

"We don't have children, John. Have you noticed that?"

"Some people don't have children, Susie."

"And I suppose I'm some people." She stopped the treadle, but kept her focus on the needle. "Am I some people, John? Am I?"

The phone jarred me awake and I realized that someone had covered me with a blanket. Morgan had answered the phone in the kitchen and was now standing in the doorway of the study.

"The sheriff's on the phone," she said.

I nodded and picked up. "Bucky?"

"John, I'm calling to tell you that we found nothing in or around the Jeep that might help."

"That's too bad," I said.

"I'm sorry about McCormack. He's a hardass, but I'm told he's good."

"I hope so." I looked out the window to see it was late afternoon and that a few flakes of snow were starting to fall. "What now?"

The sheriff was silent for a few awkward seconds. "We're still out there looking. We're radiating our search out into the desert from where we found the Jeep. We're in the air as well."

"Sounds good," I said. "I'll come out there and join in."

"Why don't you stay clear. We've got the area covered."

"Okay." I hung up.

I walked upstairs without going into the kitchen and seeing Morgan and Gus. I stood in the shower for a long time. I tried to slow my breathing, tried to clear my mind, tried to understand what was happening. I stared through the steam at the tiles of the shower wall until they didn't make sense, until their color seemed unreal. I turned off the water, half dried, and then sat on the edge of the tub. The window was steamed up and I couldn't see out, but I knew it was snowing hard. I felt it.

In the kitchen I found Gus and Morgan preparing dinner. Gus was kneading bread dough at the counter. Morgan was stirring something in a pot at the stove. I kissed her on her neck and looked over her shoulder.

"Smells good," I said.

"What now?" she asked.

I looked at Zoe and Emily sleeping in the corner. "I don't know." I glanced out at the snow. "How cold is it out there?"

"It's plenty cold," Gus said. "And it's getting colder." He left the dough and wiped his hands on a towel.

"I'm going out to walk the barns," I said. "Then I'm going to go out to look for David."

"It's dark out," Morgan said. "You can't see anything. Especially in this mess. How is getting yourself killed going to help David?"

I stood there, looking stupid.

"You need rest," Morgan said.

"I can't rest," I said.

"You're going in the morning and I'm going with you," Gus said. He eyes looked weak, but his voice was strong.

"In this weather?"

"Yep. Morgan's better with the horses and I don't mind the cold and you need somebody to keep you awake."

I glanced at Morgan. I could see that the two of them had already discussed the matter and I was stuck with their decision. "Okay, okay. I'll go out and check on everybody."

"When you come back, you're eating," Morgan said.

"Yes, ma'am," I said.

"Take the dogs with you," Gus said.

I walked through the quiet of the snow and up and down the aisles of the barns a couple of times. The dogs stayed close. Zoe had always been able to tell when I was bothered by something. As we walked back to the big barn I watched the track the three-legged coyote left in the snow. Zoe made two continuous tracks, punctuated by deep impressions of her feet. The coyote left a similar pattern, but wherever she stopped, there was a place of undisturbed or barely disturbed snow under her left forepaw. I couldn't stop thinking about it. Perhaps I was trying to imagine anything to take my mind off David, but that gap, that space, that break in her track fascinated me because it was only there briefly and only while she was still there. Once she moved on, her rear foot stamped its impression where her front one had been.

I lay there that night, unable to sleep, but desperately needing rest. I was afraid to sleep, afraid to dream. I felt Morgan drift off beside me; her breathing was a restful rhythm to me. I put my hand on her hip, perhaps to be sure she was there. I watched the sky lighten. I got dressed and went downstairs. Gus was up and waiting for me, had coffee made. He looked better than I felt. He handed me a mug.

"Drink this," he said. "I'm filling a couple of thermoses."

"Thanks."

"The snow has let up a lot. I'd say we got at least seven inches."

"That's not too bad."

"How are you holding up?" Gus asked, studying my face.

I shrugged.

The phone rang and I jumped, answered it quickly. It was Howard.

"No, nothing," I told him. "The sheriff and state police are out searching, dozens of them. They've got planes up." There were probably not dozens of searchers, but they had had planes up. "I'm going out again myself right now."

"Sylvia and I will be there tonight," he said. "We're flying into Denver and renting a car."

"Rent something with four-wheel drive," I said. "We've got snow."

He was briefly silent, then, "Okay."

"Call and let Morgan know when to expect you."

I hung up. I was not happy he and his ex-wife were coming, but that was what they should do. I wrote a note for Morgan and left it on the table.

"Let's go," Gus said.

I pulled on my jacket, then went into my study and grabbed my rifle. We walked out through the snow to the truck. I took my fly rod from the behind the seat and tossed it into the drifted snow in the bed. I then, for the first time in my life, put a rifle in my rifle rack.

I tried to keep focus, but realized I was driving the highway without scouring it. I'd traveled that stretch many times already since David's disappearance. I told Gus that since the sheriff was looking in the desert and generally west of town, we would search east, toward the reservation.

"Makes as much sense as anything," Gus said.

"Keep your eyes open for a blue BMW."

"Why?"

"A couple of rednecks. I've got a bad feeling about them."

"That's usually the way I feel about rednecks."

"These assholes picked fights with both David and me and I saw them talking to David the other day."

"You think?"

"I don't know." I shook my head. "I'm thinking everything right about now. How are you feeling?"

"I'm fine."

"You know, I appreciate privacy as much as the next guy and this might not be the best time, but how about telling me what's going on?"

"Don't worry about it."

"Gus, you look sick. Your medicine keeps changing. You sleep a lot. Tell me something. I'll find out at some point."

"I'm seventy-nine years old," he said.

"I know that."

"And I'm pretty strong for seventy-nine."

"You're very strong for seventy-nine," I said.

"I've got cancer."

"Okay." I can't say that I was stunned by the news; I'd suspected as much. Still, hearing it was hard and I felt like I had been sucker-punched. I wanted to pull off the road, but I kept driving. We came around the big curve and the valley appeared before us. "What do we do about it?" I asked. "What kind of cancer? Just what are we dealing with?"

"It's my pancreas," he said.

I didn't say anything.

"I'm dying, John." I couldn't bring myself to look at his eyes. I studied the road. "There's not much to do about it," he said. "But we can talk about this later."

"Talk about it later?"

"What's talking about it now going to accomplish?"

His point was well taken and I was left silent. As we rolled into town, I said, "I'm sorry, Gus." I was sorry he was sick, but I was also sorry I had pressed him into the admission.

"Why sorry? I'm an old man. Old men die. I swear some people would whine if you hanged them with a new rope. I'm not one of those people."

I glanced up through the windshield at the sky. "The snow's stopped."

We stopped at the diner for a couple of muffins. I saw the back of Duncan Camp's head in the rear of the restaurant and left Gus to pay for the food. Camp was sitting with three men in a booth and I could hear them as I got closer.

"So, the whole sheriff's department is out searching the desert for that cocksucker," Camp said. "And I mean that literally."

Another of the men caught sight of me and directed Camp's attention behind him toward me. Camp was stunned to see me there and was trying to figure a way to backpedal. He rose and followed me as I walked away.

"John," he said. "It ain't like that."

I turned to him. "What's it like, Duncan?"

"I was just joshing with the boys, you know." For the world, the man looked sorry.

I didn't have it in me to be angry, even disappointed. Perhaps I simply was not surprised, and that was surprising in itself.

"Listen, Duncan, I figure I need to clear out before you start with the nigger jokes. I wouldn't want to cramp your style."

"That ain't fair, John," he said as I turned away.

I faced him again. "I'm sorry it isn't fair, Duncan. That's going to eat at me for the rest of the day." I left him standing there and walked out telling Gus to come along as I passed.

I sat behind the wheel of the truck and threw my head back against the seat. I felt as if the whole world was upside-down.

"What's wrong, nephew?" Gus asked.

"You know what I am?" I asked.

"What's that?"

"I'm that three-legged coyote."

"I don't follow."

"I can't recognize my own tracks until I stop moving."

"What are you talking about?"

"Nothing."

At the gas station, I asked the attendant if she had seen the blue BMW while I paid for gas.

"Those fools," she said. She was a heavyset woman with hard, blue eyes. "They come in a lot."

"Do you know them?"

She shook her head.

"So, you wouldn't have any idea where they live?"

She took this the wrong way and her blue eyes became harder. "I said I don't know them. How would I know where they live?"

"I didn't mean anything," I said. She softened immediately. "Maybe you could tell me which way they go after they gas up?"

"Sometimes east, sometimes west."

I thanked her for her useless answer.

As I was leaving she said, "Of course, at the end of the day when they stop, they're headed east."

"Thank you."

We drove over to the reservation on the back roads, finding nothing along the way. I used the pay phone in front of the tribal office building to call Morgan. She told me that Howard had called and said that he and Sylvia would be there at eight that night. Then I put a call into the sheriff's office and learned there was nothing to know. I blew out a breath and looked up to see Daniel White Buffalo standing at the window of the truck talking to Gus.

"Anything we can do?" Daniel asked me.

"Yeah, why don't you just shoot me now," I said. "Have you seen the rednecks in the BMW?"

"You mean the neo-Nazi boys?" he said.

"That would be them," I said.

"I see them around sometimes. They're sons of bitches. Them

and their asshole friend in the dually. I think he's the one shot my cows."

"Dually?"

"Big black one. Four-wheel Ford."

"Any idea where they live?"

"Don't know, don't want to know."

"I can understand that," Gus said.

"Well, we're going to keep on driving the roads," I said.

"You should talk to Elvis Monday," Daniel said. "He got into a fight with them guys. He said he was gonna shoot them. He might know where they are. He wants to shoot everybody. He's like his mother."

"Okay, Daniel." I walked around and climbed into the truck.

"Where to?" Gus asked.

"Clara Monday's."

Elvis Monday was sitting in a chair on the porch of the modular home. He was smoking a brown cigarette. He watched as I climbed out of the truck, but didn't rise. Gus stayed in his seat. He said he was tired.

"Elvis," I greeted the man.

"Buffalo soldier," he said.

I sat on the steps with him and looked back at my truck. "How is your mother?" I asked.

"She's inside."

"Is she doing okay?"

"She's cooking. I hear your friend is missing."

"He is. White Buffalo told me you had a fight with a couple of white guys in a BMW."

"Assholes," he said. "I was going to shoot them, but ammunition is too expensive, know what I mean? I had them all set up." He aimed a pretend rifle into the yard.

"You know where they live?"

"I followed them. Assholes. All you have to do is open your nose and follow the ass smell."

"Where?"

Elvis started to say something and then stopped. "You should go in and say hello to my mother."

"I'll be right back," I said. I went to my truck, to Gus's window. "Gus, open up the jockey box and hand me that pack of cigarettes."

Gus opened the box. "What are you doing with cigarettes?" he asked.

"I just keep some for times like this. Old Clara is traditional. There's a new towel in a plastic bag under your seat. Give that to me as well. You got any money?"

"I've got a twenty," Gus said.

"Let me have it."

He did. I took the towel, the cigarettes, and the bill and walked past Elvis into the house. Clara Monday looked as old as anyone I had ever seen, but she had looked that way for fifteen years. She was a skinny stick of wrinkled muscle wound up and ready to spring. She wasn't cooking, but was sitting in front of a little black and white television. The picture was very clear. She was watching CSPAN.

"Hello, Clara. I brought you these," I said.

She looked at the gifts and nodded, gestured for me to put them on the table. Then she nodded toward the chair beside her.

"Watching the government?" I asked.

"Their government," she said. "They sure like to talk."

"Your house is looking nice."

"Thank you."

"The president is a liar," she said. "I say that because he doesn't tell the truth. I could understand if he didn't want to get caught, but he's caught anyway. Why lie when the truth is in plain view?"

"That's the way our government works," I said.

"Do you still run cows?"

"No ma'am."

"Too bad. Why not?"

"I don't like cows. I just train horses now."

She nodded.

"They get away with everything," she said, nodding to the television again.

"I guess they do."

"They just get away with it."

"Yes, ma'am."

"When you're out there, tell Elvis the house is cold," she said.

"I'll tell him." I stood and walked back out. Elvis was at the truck talking to Gus through the passenger window. He looked down and stepped back from the truck. He came around to my side as I climbed in behind the wheel. "Your mother needs some wood in the stove," I told him.

"Okay. I must do that," Elvis said. "The assholes are squatting in the old cabin up in Mouse Canyon. Not far from the creek."

"Thank you, Elvis." As we rolled away I looked over at Gus. "What was that all about?"

"What was what all about?"

"What were you two talking over?"

"Just talking."

FOURTEEN

WE DROVE EVERY BACK ROAD we could find while there was light and Gus finally asked me, "What do you plan to do with what Elvis told you?"

"I don't know."

"Are you going to tell the sheriff?"

"I don't know. I do know that it's a little dark to be messing around up in that canyon now," I said.

"I'm going up there with you," Gus said. "I know you. That's why you didn't head straight there."

I didn't say anything.

"I'm going with you."

We headed west toward home. All we had gotten for our efforts was tired and I was more than a little discouraged. In fact, I was terrified, but too much in shock to actually feel it. As we rolled down the hill to the house I saw an unfamiliar car and only then remembered that Howard and Sylvia would be there. I set the brake and looked over at Gus.

"Here we go," he said. "How are you holding up?"

"Not so well," I said.

We climbed out of the truck. Morgan came out onto the porch. Howard and Sylvia hung back inside the doorway. Morgan gave me a sympathetic touch on the shoulder and I stepped inside.

"Sylvia, Howard," I said. "I wish I could say I'm glad to see you."

"Any news?" Sylvia asked.

"No." I looked to Morgan. "Any calls?"

She shook her head.

"Well, let's sit down and I'll tell you what I know. I'm sure Morgan's told you everything, but you'll hear it again."

I sat with Sylvia and Howard in the kitchen and told them the story. Morgan and Gus went about the business of feeding the horses and checking the water. Sylvia was in shock. I could tell she would have cried if any of this made sense. Not the how of it, but the why. Howard was uncharacteristically quiet, until I glanced at him following a prolonged silence.

"You want to blame me for this," he said.

I didn't understand.

Sylvia was confused as well, looking from Howard to me, but she spoke up. "What are you talking about?"

"Tell her, John," Howard said.

I said nothing. I didn't know what to say.

Howard looked at Sylvia. "I came here for New Year's to see David and we got into a fight. He ran out and got lost in the snow. John had to find him."

"He was fine," I said.

"Yeah, that's why he needed a doctor." Howard was yelling at himself, looking to hurt himself.

"A doctor?" Sylvia tried to catch up.

"I came here with Pamela, the woman I'm planning to marry." Saying it embarrassed him.

This was news to Sylvia and it made her cough up an involuntary laugh, then her face went blank. "What about David? A doctor?"

"We had a fight, an argument, like I said, and he ran out in the snow and nearly froze to death. He was drunk and I was drunk and, yes, it was my fucking fault." He ran a hand through his hair and looked away.

"That has nothing to do with this," I said.

"What if he's just disappeared to get some attention? Maybe he's okay, just out there waiting for the fuss."

"Shut up, Howard," Sylvia said.

"Tell me it's not a possibility," Howard said. "Look me in the face and tell me it's not a possibility, Sylvia."

"It's not a possibility," I said. But I was lying. As much as it was unlikely and I didn't believe it, it was, in fact, a possibility and probably one considered by the state policeman, McCormack.

"What do we do?" Sylvia said.

"You wait," I said.

Howard huffed, a sound suggesting that he had stumbled on a way to understand it all and a way to blame someone other than himself, namely his son. I didn't like him right then any more than I had during our last meeting, but I did understand. I understood how fear was making his mind work.

"Shut up," Sylvia said to him again.

Morgan and Gus came into the mud room and kicked off their boots. Gus used a towel to wipe the dogs' feet and let them go.

Howard reached down to pet Emily. His yelp went right through me. The coyote had ripped his hand open with her teeth. It bloodied quickly. He held it to his chest and rocked back and forth.

"That son of a bitch bit me," he said.

"Let me see that," Morgan said. She peeled his good hand away and looked at the wound. "It's not bad."

"Has it had its shots?" Howard asked.

"Yes, she has," Gus said, showing no sympathy and certainly no concern. He called Emily and she followed him into the next room.

I relaxed back into my chair. I didn't have the energy for any kind of fuss. The dog had bitten Howard and that was that. There was nothing to do about it. There was no training that was going to happen that night. I didn't know what had frightened the dog to make her bite, whether it was the way he had reached down to her or his smell, his voice. The truth was I felt like biting him, too, and I recognized that as my way of dealing with the fear.

I returned to talk of David, telling Sylvia and Howard about the Jeep and where it was found, while Morgan dressed the wound. "I'm going back out tomorrow to look some more."

"Can I go with you?" Sylvia asked.

I shook my head. "You'll slow me down and I'll be worrying about you," I said. "I'm sorry to be so blunt."

"I understand," she said.

I was telling the truth, but not how she understood it. I would have been so occupied with her concern that I would not have been focused. More importantly, I expected trouble. I expected things the next day to be ugly.

"We'll wait here," Morgan said.

"It's better if you wait around here in case someone calls," I said. I looked at Morgan as she finished the bandage. I imagined her sitting around the house all day with the two of them, awkward silences and hard words, fear and nervousness.

Gus looked at me and said, "I'm going to bed. You go to bed, too. You can't be good at searching if you can't see."

I nodded.

Gus left the room.

"Gus is right. I am going to bed," I said to Sylvia and Howard.

"I've put Sylvia in the back room and Howard in the study," Morgan said. She gave me a nod of support.

"Make yourselves at home," I told them.

"I'll be right up," Morgan said.

That night Morgan and I lay in bed and we could hear the arguing whispers of Sylvia and Howard. I wondered what that car ride from Denver had been like for them. I knew how scared and upset I was, but I could not imagine their fear and confusion. Morgan stroked my forehead.

I didn't believe I could sleep, but I did. I awoke before sunrise and found Morgan still awake, still touching my brow.

"Didn't you sleep?" I asked.

"No. I wanted to be sure you slept."

"I'm scared," I said.

"I know, sweetie."

But she couldn't know all that I was scared of. I was afraid of what I might have to do. I sat up and looked out the window.

"I'll make some coffee."

"Thanks."

We dressed and walked down the stairs to find Gus in the kitchen with Sylvia. Coffee was already made and waiting.

"Did you get any rest?" Morgan asked Sylvia.

Sylvia shook her head. "I didn't try."

I looked at Sylvia's face. I had always liked her and really could never see her married to Howard. "I'm going to find him," I said. "I promise." The promise felt fat and thick in my throat and I knew I shouldn't have said it, but I was more promising myself than her. I was convincing myself that I would find David, but I still blamed myself for his being missing.

As we rolled away from the house in the truck, light just finding the sky, Gus commented on how bad he felt for Sylvia and Howard. Then he apologized for the coyote biting Howard.

"I probably have been a little lax on the training."

I waved him off. "Emily's fine," I said. She did what she's programmed to do when she's scared. Howard was scared, so she got scared."

In town, the deputy Hanks was just getting out of his rig as we drove by the station house. I rolled down my window and called to him.

"Any news?" I asked.

He looked cold, maybe nervous. "Bucky was planning to call you this morning," he said.

"Oh, yeah?"

"McCormack is cutting off the search," he said, flatly, then looked as if he shouldn't have spoken.

"Why is that?" I felt hollow.

"I guess he doesn't think we can find him. Mr. Hunt, we covered damn near the whole desert. We didn't even find a track."

I didn't say anything. Gus was looking away out his window.

"What's the sheriff say?" I asked. "I mean, does he agree with McCormack?"

"I guess. Listen, he'll tell you himself. He told McCormack about that guy getting lost in the woods and McCormack listened. Just talk to Bucky."

I nodded and watched the lanky deputy walk away.

"Mouse Canyon?" Gus asked.

"Mouse Canyon."

Mouse Canyon was on the northern edge of the reservation. A narrow, rugged canyon, it was dry enough that no one cared to go there. Part of it had burned ten years ago and no one had gone to put out the fire. The new growth was thick and low. There was a small creek that managed to flow year round, but supported few fish, probably because of ranching, but no one remembered there ever being fish there. The road was deeply rutted, but not terrible, perhaps because of the lack of traffic and perhaps because the county didn't attempt to maintain it. I had seen the line shack that Elvis described long ago and knew that it was well up near the end of the road. I wondered how anyone could get a BMW up there. A quarter-mile up the road that question was answered.

"Why are you stopping?" Gus asked.

I pointed.

"What?"

Look harder. I got out of the truck and Gus followed me. The BMW was dressed in a green car tarp and covered with branches, fairly well hidden. I looked at the road. "Look here. Dually tracks."

"It would seem they're at home," Gus said.

We climbed back into the truck.

"Are you sure you're up to this?" I asked the old man. In fact, I believed he was more up to it than I was.

"Just drive."

I recalled that the cabin was well up the canyon, so I stopped about a mile in. I turned to Gus and said, "I want you to stay here."

"Why?"

"If I'm not back in an hour, go get the sheriff."

I climbed out of the truck and reached in for my rifle. I studied Gus's face and waited for his argument, but none came. "You okay?"

He nodded.

"Let me have that roll of duct tape from the jockey box."

He handed me the tape.

"Thanks."

"An hour," he said.

"Then you go for help."

I walked away up the road and didn't glance back at him. The sky was cloudless and blue. I unzipped my jacket, then felt for shells in my pocket. My heart was racing, but all this seemed correct. Sometimes things were just simple, I thought. The people you expected to do the bad thing did the bad thing. I believed the rednecks had done something to David and I was going to find out. Maybe I should have called the sheriff, but I didn't know whom I could trust.

Not quite a mile from my truck I heard the thumping of a motor, a generator. I approached through the brush and saw the cabin. It didn't look as run down as I'd remembered. A black dually pickup was parked in front next to a defunct propane tank. Smoke came from the metal pipe chimney and was carried away from me with the wind. Then I became concerned that being upwind they could smell me. I realized I was thinking too much. I ducked down as I spotted the flash of a head in the window. I asked myself what I was doing there. The scene felt surreal. It wasn't so much that I was scared, but I didn't feel like I was standing on anything. I moved to the rear of the house and listened, but all I could hear was the generator. I kept low and made my way around the side to the front corner. I stood erect and was startled by a man. It was the larger of the two men with whom I had fought. He was holding a toothbrush in his hand. He started to back away.

"I wouldn't run," I said, leveling the barrel of my rifle at him. "I just wouldn't run."

"What—"

"I wouldn't talk either," I said. I shook my head. "No sounds. Throw down the toothbrush." He did. "Now turn around and remember that there's a rifle aimed at your back."

I followed him into the cabin.

"That was quick," a man said to him. "What's wrong with you?"

I stepped inside.

"What the fuck?" This was another man I had never seen. The shirtless man moved toward a counter near him and I fired a round through the metal roof. He stopped, stood straight. He had red hair and a red beard and a left sleeve of tattoos. His right arm was bare.

"Sit around the table," I said. "All of you. Now."

"Nigger, you done fucked up now," the wiry man whom I had punched said. "You done fucked up bad."

They sat in the wooden chairs and I walked around the room. On the far wall was large Nazi flag. There was a pistol on the counter, a .357. I flipped open the chamber and let the shells fall onto the floor, then I tossed the gun through the window, breaking the glass. I took the roll of tape from my pocket. I nudged the back of the smallest man's head with the tip of the barrel. "Okay, weasel, tape up your friends. Start with the redhead."

"Fuck you," he said.

I poked him with the tip hard. He cried out and I did it again.

"Hey, fuckwad," the redhead said. "We could just rush you. You can't shoot all three of us with that thing."

"I think I can," I said. "But if I don't we're going to be slipping around fighting in your friend's blood and brains." I poked the little guy again. "Take the tape."

He took it, then stood, rubbing the back of his head. "Tape their hands together behind their backs, wrap some around their arms and strap their feet to the chair legs."

"I'm going to kill you, you fucking nigger," he said, as began tap-ing his running buddy instead of the redhead, but I let him continue.

"You're not much for talking your way out of a mess, are you?" I said.

"What do you want?" the redhead asked.

"I'm looking for a friend," I said.

"I'll be your friend," the little one said. He was finished with the first man and moved to the redhead.

"You know this is going to go on your permanent record," the redhead said.

I smiled and nodded.

The small man stood up and away from the table. I gestured for him to have a seat.

"Are you going to put your gun down and tie me up now?" he asked.

"I think I'll just let you sit for a while. So, have you men seen my friend? He's about twenty, brown hair. A white guy."

"Haven't seen him," red said.

"Are you sure? I ask because I believe this watch on the counter is his."

"My mother gave me that watch," the little man said.

"That's a lie," I said. "We all know you didn't have a mother."

"I think you should put that rifle down and tie me up," the wea-sel said.

"Yeah," said the man I'd met outside.

"Where is my friend?" I asked.

"Fuck you," from the redhead. "I ain't telling you shit."

"Your friend is a fucking pussy," the weasel said. "He didn't even fight back. 'Please don't hurt me, please don't hurt me.' Fucking fag-got. At least the other faggot fought."

I was lost in anger. But I knew now that they had, in fact, taken David. I didn't know if he was alive or dead and I was sick about it. I didn't know what to do next, what to say it, how to say it. I'd ex-hausted my tough-guy act.

Gus entered the cabin.

"Fuck me," the redhead said. "What is this? Nigger heaven?"

What happened next was and still is a blur. I recall a flash and a loud pop and the red beard expanding and breaking, the chair falling over, the weasel sliding across the floor to the wall and Gus, standing there, a .45 in his hand.

"Fuck, fuck, fuck," the remaining tied-up man kept saying.

"Nephew," Gus said, "tape that piece of shit to a chair."

I grabbed the weasel by his hair and pulled him to a chair, started wrapping him up. I was slowly coming to my senses, understanding what had just happened. "You killed him," I said.

"It would seem so," Gus said.

The little man still hadn't said anything while his friend kept saying *fuck*.

"You killed him, Gus," I said again.

"I've got two left," the old man said.

At first I thought he was talking about bullets, but I then realized he meant the men. Gus's face was tired, hard.

Gus pointed his pistol at the weasel's face. "Where is David?" he asked. "You'll tell me or I'll shoot you. Then I'll point the gun at your buddy. Where is David?"

"He's up the canyon," the man said.

"Alive?" I asked.

"I don't know."

"Where up the canyon?" I asked, but I couldn't take my eyes off the dead man, his face flattened in his own blood.

"There's a trail just after the creek that leads to a hole in a big rock. I think somebody blasted out a place to keep supplies or something. He's in there."

"He'd better be," Gus said. "If my nephew comes back here alone, I'm going to shoot you. Do you understand?"

"That's where he is."

I looked at Gus. He blew out a breath, then leaned against the wall. He was sick.

"Go," he said.

"How far away is the trail?"

"A mile maybe. But he's probably dead. Jesus, man, don't shoot me."

"Was he dead when you left him?" I asked.

"No."

"He'd better not be dead," Gus said.

"Where are the keys to that truck?" I asked the weasel.

"In the ignition."

I ran out to the dually, climbed in and drove up the canyon, looking for the creek. I saw it, stopped, and walked back and forth looking for the trail. When I finally saw it, it was clear to see and I wondered if all of this was making me blind. I couldn't believe that Gus had shot that man. Then I couldn't believe that I had put myself in a place where I could have shot him. I didn't know what was going to happen. How were we going to explain the death of a bound man?

I followed the trail across the frozen creek and, about a hundred yards in, saw the depression in the big rock. It opened like a cave, but was obviously the result of blasting. It got dark pretty quickly, but it wasn't pitch. I didn't have a light and so I moved slowly, letting my eyes adjust as I went.

My foot hit something. Not a rock. It was a body. I didn't think, I just grabbed the legs and dragged the body to the opening and the light. It was David and he was beaten badly. His eyes were closed, his mouth pulp, but he was breathing. He was breathing. I untied his hands and feet. I talked to him, but I couldn't tell if he could hear me. His arm was badly broken, bending off at a bizarre angle once untied and I tried to straighten it over his chest. He was bruised and bloody everywhere and I just knew he was bleeding inside. I started to cry. I didn't know whether to leave him and get help or try to carry him to the truck. I couldn't leave him, I decided. I simply couldn't. If he was going to die, he wasn't going to die alone. I dragged him as gently as I could back along the trail and across the ice to the truck. I struggled with his limp body and got him into the bed.

I drove back to the cabin and found Gus nearly asleep as he leaned against the wall. The men were still tied and Gus still held the pistol, but he looked bad.

"Gus, come on, I've got David in the truck."

"You can't leave us here," the weasel said.

Neither Gus nor I responded to him or even looked his way. He was still shouting when we were outside.

Gus took control of the situation again. "Drive us back to the truck," he said. "I'll ride in the back with David." He whistled as he observed the man. "They did a number on you, son."

I drove us back to my truck.

Gus said, "Let's put David in the cab. He can't ride in the back. It's just too cold."

We gingerly moved David from the bed of the dually and over to the seat of my truck.

"Do you want to get in on this side or through the driver's door?" I asked Gus and realized I was shaking.

Gus gave me a hard look and I felt the differences in our years and experiences. He put his hand on my shoulder and said, "Take David to the hospital. Tell the cops you found David anywhere but here or near here."

"What are you talking about?"

"Just do it. We don't have time to argue."

I got into the truck and looked at David, slumped over, his head almost to my thigh. He looked so bad I couldn't believe it. I started the truck and made my way out of the canyon, holding him as still as possible with my right hand. I pulled the truck out onto the highway and picked up some speed. The blood matted in David's hair was dark and angry.

At the emergency room, David was taken away from me and I called home and then the sheriff. I sat in a stiff plastic chair and waited. Bucky arrived within minutes, sat beside me.

"How is he?" the sheriff asked, pressing his back into the chair. I was actually impressed that that was his first question. I was expecting him to immediately want to know where I had found him.

"He's in bad shape, Bucky."

We sat for a few seconds.

"Want to tell me where you found him?"

I'd been constructing my lie all the way to the hospital. "Believe it or not he was lying in a ditch about ten miles west of town. Between here and my place. I wasn't even looking yet and there he was."

The sheriff blew out a breath, then bit at his thumbnail.

"He's been beaten really badly."

"Is he conscious?"

"He wasn't," I said. "I don't know about now."

There was a haze between us, but I sensed that he didn't believe I was lying or somehow didn't care. The latter made little sense to me.

We sat and waited.

"How is your uncle?" he asked.

"Okay, I guess."

"I guess McCormack will be glad to hear David turned up," Bucky said.

"David's parents are driving here with Morgan," I said.

He nodded.

We waded through some more silence.

"I hope he's okay," Bucky said.

"Me, too."

"Alongside the road," he said.

"In the ditch."

Morgan, Sylvia, and Howard came through the doors just as the doctor came out to talk to me.

"The young man suffered massive internal injuries," the doctor said.

"How is he?" Howard asked.

"The beating he took about his head." The doctor paused. "There was a lot of trauma to the brain."

I could see how upset the doctor was. She was not used to this sort of thing and I thought as I watched her that no one should be.

"He's gone," she said.

Sylvia crumpled and I caught her. Bucky backed away from the scene. I reached out and took Howard's hand. Morgan was crying and we locked eyes. She whispered that she loved me, then looked away.

"I want to see him," Sylvia said.

"I don't think that's a good idea," the doctor said.

"She's right," I said.

"Who could do this?" Sylvia cried.

Sylvia and Howard sat in the plastic chairs and shared their grief.

"Where's Gus?" Morgan asked.

"He's around," I said.

We all drove back to my house in Morgan's car. Morgan put Sylvia to bed and Howard sat in the kitchen staring at a bottle of wine he refused to open. I kept wanting to leave and go back to find Gus, but I didn't say anything. Morgan came into my study and closed the door.

"Where's Gus?" she asked.

"Over by the reservation," I said. "That's where we found David. Gus killed a man today. I think he's up there killing all of them." I found it odd how easily those words came from my mouth.

"Oh, my god."

"He told me to lie to the sheriff, but what sense does that make? I've got to go back up there. I should have gone from the hospital."

Morgan was stunned. She didn't know what to say and I didn't know how to have it make any more sense for her. It made no sense to me.

A truck slid to a stop outside. Morgan and I got up and stepped out onto the porch. Gus was getting out of Elvis Monday's pickup. Gus was unsteady and I ran over to support him. I glanced into the truck at Elvis, asking with my eyes just what was going on.

"How is the boy?" Elvis asked.

"He died," I said.

Elvis looked straight ahead out his windshield. "I am sorry to hear that."

"Yeah."

"What's going on?" I asked, directly.

"Talking is over," Gus said.

"This is the frontier, cowboy," Elvis said. "Everyplace is the frontier. Take care of your uncle."

I nodded and stepped away.

PERCIVAL EVERETT is Professor of English at the University of Southern California. He lives outside Los Angeles and on Vancouver Island, British Columbia.

The text of *Wounded* has been set in Chaparral Pro, a typeface designed by Carol Twombly. Book design by Wendy Holdman. Composition by Prism Publishing Center. Manufactured by Maple-Vail Book Manufacturing on acid-free paper.